Linc

Dm

THE IMPOSSIBLE DREAM

THE IMPOSSIBLE DREAM

Hilary Wilde

CHIVERS

| British Library Cataloguing in Publication Data available |

This Large Print edition published by BBC Audiobooks Ltd, Bath, 2010.
Published by arrangement with the Author's Estate .

U.K. Hardcover ISBN 978 1 408 45736 8
U.K. Softcover ISBN 978 1 408 45737 5

Printed and bound in Great Britain by
CPI Antony Rowe, Chippenham and Eastbourne

CHAPTER I

As the schooner slowly approached the opening in the coral reef, Megan Crane could see the jetty, crowded with people. The water was the wonderful deep blue of the Indian Ocean, the sky cloudless, even the wind was warm against her cheeks. The town looked small, with the little houses huddled together as if seeking the sanctuary offered by the tall mountains towering above them.

'Well,' Miss Wilmot by her side said, 'here we are. I wonder if Mr Lambert himself will come and meet us. I doubt it, as we're not the V.I.P.s he honours.'

Megan Crane turned to look at the tall, slim woman with her elaborately-dressed hair. 'You don't like Craig Lambert?' Megan asked.

The words were impulsive and after she had said them Megan regretted it. Her hands tightened round the rail of the ship. Nor did she like Craig Lambert, she thought angrily, for he was ruining her brother Patrick— deliberately, too.

Then why was she here, she asked herself, on the way out to this island near the Seychelles, to work for Mr Lambert?

She smiled wryly. What choice had she? She looked at the white-flecked waves. She'd had no choice. Her father had thrown her out, so

1

she had needed the job badly. In addition, though she and Patrick had shared little love with one another, at least he was her brother, and if she could find a way to help him . . .

Miss Wilmot, Mr Lambert's P.A. who looked after his affairs in England when he was away, smiled. 'What a question,' she said. 'I work for him. Surely that's answer enough?'

'I wonder,' Megan replied.

The schooner was rolling gently as it waited outside the reef opening. The lagoon they could see was not large and a schooner was anchored by the jetty already.

Suddenly Megan's fears had to be put into words. 'Miss Wilmot,' she asked, her hair, honey-coloured and long, swinging as she turned her head, 'how will I get on? What is Mr Lambert like to work for? As I've told you, I had no real training as a dancer, even less as a dance teacher.' She tried to laugh. 'I'm really worried. Why did I get the job?'

Clara Wilmot looked at the anxious girl by her side and gave an odd smile. 'Your Mrs Arbuthnot gave you a good reference. She's known you for years, I gather. Also . . .' her mouth twisted into an even more cynical smile, 'you appear to have made a good impression on Mr Lambert.'

'Did I?' Megan found herself laughing. 'If you'd known how I felt at that time! My whole life had been turned upside down. I'd been looking after my father for four years, thinking

2

he needed me and what a good daughter I was being, then—quite suddenly—he told me I was a burden, that if I could find a job and a bed-sitter, it would solve his problem. I didn't know what to do for . . . well, I wasn't trained for anything, going straight from school to look after Dad . . .' She paused, watching the small launch that was skimming over the lagoon, leaving a wake of white beauty behind it. 'Then Mrs Arbuthnot said a *gentleman* had been making enquiries for a dancing mistress for an exclusive school and she thought I would be suitable. I couldn't believe it. Anyhow, he came one day. Luckily I didn't know he was there, because he watched me give several lessons.' Megan laughed again. 'If I'd known he was there, I'd have made an awful mess of it, for I'd have been petrified. Then I met him and he asked me the strangest questions. They seemed to have nothing to do with the job.'

'Mr Lambert is like that,' Clara Wilmot said slowly. 'He's more interested in his employees' characters than their credentials. After all, he has to be careful because this is an exclusive school. We often get children from abdicated or thrown-out European royal families as well as the very rich. We have to protect the children from unwanted publicity . . . or I should say we have, but it's not been so easy since Gaston Duval took over.'

'Gaston Duval?' Megan repeated slowly.

3

She had read Patrick's desperate letter to his father, asking for financial help, mentioning a friend who was away or there would have been no need for this appeal. Could Gaston be the friend? Megan wondered.

The launch was coming fast towards them, she saw. Would Mr Lambert be in it? she wondered. No, she decided, it could be the pilot. Perhaps the opening in the coral reef was tricky.

'Gaston Duval and Craig Lambert are enemies,' Clara Wilmot was saying slowly. 'Like their fathers were, and their grandfathers. It's a family feud. Gaston wants the island to become a world-famous holiday-place.'

'Yes,' Megan agreed. 'I remember when Patrick and Georgina came out . . .'

'Patrick Crane . . .' Miss Wilmot said slowly, her voice rising, her face changing as she turned to look at the girl by her side. 'Is he a relation of yours?'

'My brother.' A faintly defiant note crept into Megan's voice. Though she didn't love Patrick, she was allowing no one to run him down!

'Why on earth didn't I . . . The name—I should have thought . . .' Miss Wilmot sounded agitated, unusual, for normally she was not only efficient but impersonal. Now she began to look angry. 'Did you tell Mr Lambert?' she asked.

4

'Of course.' Megan was puzzled. 'As soon as I knew where the Lambert School was, I told Mr Lambert my brother lived on the island.'

'And what, if I may ask, was his reaction?'

Megan frowned. She had a fey look in many ways, with the cloud of hair that kept falling over her face, the unhappy eyes, the wistful smile.

'Well, in a way, he wasn't very pleased.'

'I'm not surprised,' Miss Wilmot almost snapped.

Megan's hands clenched. 'And why not?' she demanded.

'Your brother and his wife are part of the island's lesser-liked population. They're friends of Gaston Duval. That alone is damning.'

Megan nodded silently—so Gaston Duval *was* Patrick's friend.

'What did Mr Lambert say when you told him?' Clara Wilmot asked, her voice crisp.

'Nothing, really. It was the way his eyes narrowed as he stared at me. He asked me if that was why I had applied for the post, but when I said I hadn't even known where the school was and that Mrs Arbuthnot had arranged everything, Mr Lambert seemed to relax.'

'He believed you?' Clara Wilmot gave a strange laugh and Megan blushed.

'Well, it was the truth.'

'Maybe, but he doesn't usually. Still, maybe

5

he has a reason. Craig Lambert does nothing without a reason. By the way, in case you meet Gaston Duval, watch out. He's said to be most charming, but knowing him could cost you your job. Gaston is said to be very handsome and Craig Lambert . . .'

'Is the ugliest man I know,' Megan said angrily. What right had Craig Lambert to lay down laws about who she could know? It was true, as well, that Craig *was* ugly—a strange ugliness that attracted you against your will. Would she ever forget the first time she met him, introduced by Mrs Arbuthnot? A tall man with incredibly broad shoulders, a sun-tanned skin, square chin, high forehead, dark haircut too short by modern standards, and a grave, unsmiling face. He had stared at her thoughtfully, narrowing his eyes in that sceptical way, and she had seen the mole on his cheek. His voice had impressed her: a deep vibrant voice, full of life and strength. And impatience.

'Is that so? I had no idea,' a deep, vibrant but amused voice asked. It was Craig Lambert himself.

Megan swung round. She had forgotten about the launch, but as she looked about her wildly, seeking the right words to say, which in any case would be quite inadequate, for she had been unforgivably rude, she saw there was no sign of the launch. So Craig Lambert *had* come to meet her.

6

'I . . . I . . .' she began nervously, looking up at the grave-faced man staring at her. He was wearing a thin white suit.

Miss Wilmot, always tactful, came to her rescue.

'I didn't expect you to meet us, Mr Lambert,' she said. 'It's nice of you.'

'You won't think so in a minute,' he said dourly. 'Someone had to meet Miss Crane, because you're going back immediately. The schooner is waiting, so . . .'

'But I thought . . .' the elegantly-dressed, so composed Miss Wilmot, in her pale pink shantung suit, looked as if she was going to cry, Megan thought.

'So did I. Sorry,' Craig Lambert said quickly, but not as if he really meant it. 'Things have changed. That merger with Cox is important and something has come up, so I need you on the spot. You know as much about it as I do, perhaps more. You can come out another time.' He moved his hand impatiently, as if brushing away her disappointment. 'We're going ashore in the launch as I have to get Miss Wilmot on the schooner that's waiting for her,' he said with equal curtness to the silent Megan, whose red cheeks had returned to their usual colour, but who still felt horrified at what she had said and he had heard. It was hardly, she was thinking, a good start to a job she was afraid she didn't qualify for.

7

He led the way to the waiting launch. Only Miss Wilmot's luggage was to be taken.

'Miss Crane's will come later,' Craig said curtly.

The launch bounced about in the rough waves which came roaring to break up on the coral reef, but once through the narrow opening, the water was as smooth as any village pond. Craig Lambert was talking briskly to Miss Wilmot, who looked slightly green but was dutifully making notes of what he told her. No one looked at Megan, so she sat very still, grateful because she wanted the chance to look at the land that was going to be her new home . . . for as long as she could keep the job!

As they came closer to the island, she could see how beautiful it was. So much colour. Trees with huge red flowers, arches covered with purple blossoms, the dark-skinned men crowded on the jetty wore white trousers and sleeveless shirts as well as straw hats, but the women, crowding with them, seemed all to be wearing bright crimson or vivid yellow dresses.

Palm trees were standing along the quayside, their slender trunks bent as if the wind had pushed them down for so many years that they had given up the fight. To Megan, palm trees meant so much. They were part of her impossible dream.

'*The impossible dream,*' she said silently, staring at the island before her. The dream she

8

had so often had in her life. Oddly enough, usually after an un-happy day, and—looking back—she realised just what a lot of unhappy days she had had in her twenty years of life. Always there had been this impossible dream—that one day she would live on an island where palm trees were silhouetted against the mountains, where the ocean came racing in, tossing fountains of sun-kissed water in the air as it hit the coral reefs, then coves of white soft sand that caressed your skin while the sun browned it, the exciting deep blue sea where strange fish lived, and trees full of chattering monkeys and tiny, brightly coloured birds hovering over flowers . . .

She had seen the *island* so often, getting brochures from travel agents and keeping the chosen picture hidden from Patrick's curious eyes. Sometimes she had decided on Barbados, or Jamaica, or the Canaries, but never, somehow, had she thought of the Seychelles. Yet here she was.

It had been Mrs Arbuthnot who reminded her on that terrible day, when the rain poured down and a gale blew along Hastings' front, and her father had just told her Patrick, her brother, was in trouble. Patrick always was in trouble, she had thought rebelliously. Patrick could do no wrong. But this, it seemed, was serious. He needed the money urgently.

How worried her father had looked! 'If only you had a good job, Meg, and could live on

9

your own, in a bed-sitter, perhaps, then I could sell this house,' her father had said.

She had felt frozen with shock. 'But what about you?'

He had nodded. Apparently it had all been arranged and nothing said to her, yet her father must have known this would happen, for he went on: 'Your Aunt Lily wants me to live with her. She's bought this cottage in Dorset, but says it's very isolated and she would like a man around.'

'But you and Aunt Lily . . .' Megan had begun, pausing again as her father looked at her. He was doing this for Patrick, she knew. Patrick who could do no wrong. Yet Dad had never got on with deaf Aunt Lily who rarely stopped grumbling.

'Perhaps Mrs Arbuthnot could help you find a job, Meg?' her father had suggested. 'One with a better salary, full time.'

Now, as the launch approached the jetty, Megan could remember the frozen desolation she had felt that day as she hurried to Mrs Arbuthnot's College of Dancing, running through the rain, stumbling through puddles, bent as she went along the Front, battling with the high winds racing across the Channel. Mrs Arbuthnot had been sympathetic. It was then she had told Megan about the *gentleman* who had been to see her, having heard high praise of her dancing college.

'You might just do, Megan,' Mrs Arbuthnot

had said excitedly. 'One door closes and another opens. Perhaps this is your impossible dream? I just can't understand your father— after all you've done for him, given up your dancing, your schooling, just to look after him and yet he can treat you like this.'

'He's never loved me,' Megan had told her. 'Aunt Lily said it was because I killed my mother.'

How angry Mrs Arbuthnot had been! Her cheeks bright red, her eyes flashing. 'Your Aunt Lily! Look, your mother was told to have no more children after Patrick was born. She should never have had you. But you didn't *ask* to be born. I blame them. They should have been more careful.'

'Are you all right, Miss Crane?' Craig Lambert's harsh voice penetrated Megan's dreams. 'You're very quiet.'

She jerked back to the present, to the launch that had drawn up by the jetty, with Miss Wilmot being helped out and Mr Lambert scowling.

'I'm sorry, Mr Lambert. I was thinking . . .'

'I'm not surprised,' he said. 'You must have a lot to think about. Come along, I haven't all day,' he added.

He helped her climb the ladder, and then she was surrounded by the chattering, laughing Creoles who had crowded the jetty, many laden with hand-made goods they hoped to sell. Mr Lambert spoke to them curtly, in a

11

strange kind of French that Megan found hard to translate, then he turned to her.

'Wait here while I get Miss Wilmot settled.'

The tall, elegantly-dressed woman shook hands with Megan formally, but Miss Wilmot had a shocked look as if her surprise and disappointment was still upsetting her.

'Goodbye.' Miss Wilmot looked round and saw that Craig Lambert was striding down the jetty, the people moving out of his way, much as waves seem to do as a launch prances through them. 'Good luck,' Clara Wilmot said quietly. 'You'll need it.'

Feeling dismayed, Megan stood very still, staring at Miss Wilmot's straight back as she hurried away.

Why was she going to need good luck? And why had Mr Lambert given her the job if he disliked Patrick? Was he going to use her as a weapon against Patrick? That was another question, but it was absurd. How could he hurt Patrick through the sister Patrick had never loved? Yet perhaps—indeed, of course, Mr Lambert couldn't know that.

What sort of man was she going to work for, anyhow? Curt, dominant, impatient, arrogant and, apparently, ruthless, according to Patrick.

She could no longer see Miss Wilmot, who had not turned for a final wave, so Megan looked at the island. The islanders, obviously respecting whatever it was Mr Lambert had said to them, kept away from her, talking to

12

one another excitedly, with laughter filling the air.

How lovely it could be living here, Megan thought, relaxing as she leant against the railing of the jetty. It was hot, but not too humid, and the slight breeze caressed her cheeks with a pleasant warmth. She looked at the small town. How crowded and small were the stone-made houses. They all seemed huddled round a centre square where there was a large white cross. Then the road seemed to vanish in a mass of trees and start to climb the mountains that sheltered the valley. On the mountainside she could see tiny houses clinging to the soil, some cattle grazing and several waterfalls so far away that the water looked like a silver pencil line down the green grass.

'Well?' The deep vibrant voice made her jump as Craig Lambert joined her. 'What do you think of it?'

Megan's hair swung as she turned her head. Her cheeks were flushed from the heat, her eyes shining with excitement.

'It's very beautiful.'

'Good. Not that you'll come here often. Of course, you'll want to visit your brother. That can be arranged. Are you very close to one another?' he asked curtly, starting to walk away.

She had almost to run to keep up with him, for his strides were long, quick and apparently

13

effortless. She had always prided herself on being a good fast walker, but this was no . . . nor could she hear all he was saying as he spoke over his shoulder.

'Not . . . very,' she managed to say.

'I see. Not a close brother-sister relationship. Just as well, perhaps. We prefer to keep the girls out of certain parts of the island. Lately so much has deteriorated. Unfortunately there has been little I could do about it, but now,' his voice sounded triumphant, 'things are going to change.'

She wondered what he meant. Was the destruction of poor Patrick part of Craig Lambert's plans?

A huge white Rolls was waiting for them. The chauffeur, dark-skinned, wearing a smart green uniform, opened the car doors. This had never been part of the dream, she thought, a Rolls-Royce! White, too!

The chauffeur drove slowly. He had little choice, for the narrow main street was crowded with cars, cyclists, and a kind of chair on wheels, drawn by a Creole running in the shafts and which carried two people. Everywhere there was colour. The shop windows sparkled with scintillating swinging toys or the bright green or purple materials, draped round dummies. The pavements were crowded, too, and no one seemed to be in a hurry. Nor did any of them look alike, for she saw Chinese faces, Indian, Creole as well as

14

white skins.

It was as if Craig Lambert read her mind. 'We have a real international mixture here. These islands were invaded so often in the past, leaving behind these souvenirs.' He gave a strange smile that seemed to relax his stern face.

They drove past the White Cross where wreaths of flowers were leaning against it, and then, as they left the town behind, the road became emptier and their passage faster. It was fascinating, Megan thought, as she looked eagerly on every side. All these colours ; all the trees and bushes seemed ablaze with brightly coloured blossoms. As the road twisted and turned to take the steep mountain gradually, she looked at the funny little houses and the small children waving and she waved back; sometimes there were groups of women, their skirts tucked round their waists as they walked into the narrow streams to wash their clothes.

As the car took a slow turn on a miniature plateau, Megan caught her breath. She could now see the other side of the town and stretching up in the middle of this small group of buildings was what looked like a thick finger reaching up towards the sky. It was so hideous, so out of keeping with the quiet beauty of the island that it shocked her.

'What's that?' she asked impulsively.

'Hotel Anglais. Run by Gaston Duval,' Craig Lambert said sharply. 'You've heard of

15

him?'

She hesitated for a moment, but there was no point in lying.

'Yes, I . . .'

'Met him?' Craig Lambert snapped.

'Of course not.' She was annoyed by his way of throwing questions sharply at her. 'How could I? I've never been here before.'

'That's as may be, but Gaston Duval gets round the world quite a bit. Your brother's dancing school, by the way, is quite near the hotel.'

'Is it?' She wondered what was best to say and decided to say as little as possible.

'Your brother and you are not good friends?' Craig Lambert asked abruptly.

Megan felt the surge of loyalty rising inside her.

'I didn't say that. I said . . . well, we are friends, but that's all.'

'Why don't you get on better?' Perhaps he saw the look on Megan's face, for he lifted a phone from his side of the car and gave instructions in the strange French he had used on the jetty. The chauffeur, sitting very upright as he drove, nodded and at the next *plateau,* always placed where a severely sharp turn came, drove off into a narrow side road which the trees lined, their leaves meeting overhead so that it was like a cathedral, and there was a green light as the sun was shut out. Then, as they turned a corner, Megan saw the most

16

beautiful view. The trees had gone, save for a few palm trees on a lawn, underneath which were some tables. The small square house was half hidden by purple flowers.

'I'm having coffee, or would you prefer a cold drink?' he asked curtly as he led the way to one of the tables, settling Megan in a chair. 'My favourite view.'

'It's beautiful. Coffee, please.'

'Black or white?' he asked.

'White, please.' Megan, leaning on the table, rested her face on her hands, as she stared at the view before her. The blue ocean spreading away. There were no quiet coves below here, just the ocean speeding in, rushing madly towards the rocks, tossing as if furious with the world. It was so . . . so . . .

'Why don't you like your brother?' Craig Lambell's curt voice jerked her back to the present.

'I didn't say I didn't *like* him,' Megan said, giving him a quick glance, for she wondered why he had suggested stopping here. Surely they could have had coffee at the school?

'No, but you implied it. Look, there are some questions I want to ask you. It's simpler here than at the school, because I'm always busy there.'

Megan looked away quickly. What sort of questions, she wondered. She must be careful what she said—in case it affected Patrick.

'Excuse me a moment,' she said. 'I just want

17

to look at this lovely view.'

She walked across the lawn to where a wall had been built of rocks. Leaning against it, she found she could look down on the small town they had recently left. How tiny it looked, she thought. Why, the houses were more like a group of children's dolls' houses and the yachts so still in the smooth lagoon looked like little paper toys.

'Are you jealous of your brother?' The words, close to her ears, made her jump. She turned quickly and found Craig Lambert by her side, leaning on the wall.

'Jealous?' She was really startled. Never had she thought of herself as being jealous, but . . .

She looked up and found Craig Lambert's eyes were narrowed thoughtfully. He was not smiling, so it was not a joke.

'I . . . well . . .' she began, then nodded. 'I suppose I am,' she said. 'My mother died when I was born and my father never forgave me. He adored Patrick. He'd do anything . . .' She stopped abruptly. Perhaps it would be unwise to let Craig Lambert know about Patrick's recent desperate cry for financial help?

'That's unusual. Usually the father adores his daughters, and it's the son who gets neglected.' He paused and again, suddenly, his question seemed to jump at her: 'Why did you want a new job so badly?'

'Be . . . because . . .' Megan began, then paused. Had she to answer these questions?

18

she asked herself. Had he the right to expect her to do so? Had he the right, even, to ask them? Maybe he had, though, for—as Miss Wilmot had said—his responsibilities at the school were terrific and that was why he was more interested in his employees' characters than their abilities.

'Why?' she repeated slowly. 'Well, it all came as rather a shock to me. My father wanted to go and live with my aunt in Dorset . . . She lives in a lonely part and said she needed a man about the house. She's very deaf and nervous and I suppose she thought a man would keep vandals away. Not that I can see poor Dad doing much,' Megan went on, her voice wistful. 'He has this wretched arthritis and is always losing balance. He's so afraid of falling that he hardly dares to walk anywhere.'

'So you had to find a job? You like your aunt?'

Again Megan hesitated. 'Yes and no. She's deaf and rather difficult. She looked after us for all my life and nothing anyone did was ever right. Then when . . . when . . .'

'You were sixteen when she left you,' Craig Lambert finished for her. 'I understand you had to leave school, though you had a promising future, and also had to give up dancing. You like dancing?'

A little puzzled, wondering how he could know so much, Megan nodded. 'We were all dancers, you see. Mother and Dad danced a lot, and often won international competitions. They were really good. Then she died and he began to get this wretched arthritis. So did . . .' Megan paused, not sure if it was wise or not to mention her brother. Yet Patrick's name could not be left out without it seeming strange. 'Patrick and Georgina danced a lot and won prizes. I also had a partner.'

'What was his name?'

The question startled her, because she hadn't thought of her one-time partner for ages. 'Reggie . . . Reggie Blake.'

'You still meet him?'

'No.' She was even more puzzled, since she couldn't see what connection it had with her job. 'He was furious when I said I couldn't go on dancing. You see, you have to practise all the time and be free to travel about, and I just couldn't leave Dad alone. He had this dreadful fear of falling down and breaking a hip.'

'So you gave up dancing, too,' Craig Lambert said thoughtfully, then turned to look at her. 'Willingly?' he asked.

'Willingly?' Puzzled, Megan had repeated the word.

'Yes. I mean was it your idea or did your father have to ask you to give up dancing?'

'He didn't know why I stopped. Of course I didn't tell him. He wouldn't have liked it at all. He's very independent in many ways. I had no choice as far as I could see it. Dad needed me—and that was all.'

20

'I see. Oh, the coffee's come. We'd better go and drink it,' Craig Lambert said, leading the way back to the table. 'I can't help wondering what made your father suddenly decide to live with your aunt. Did they get on well together? Would she be a good nurse?'

Megan hesitated again. Whatever happened, she wasn't going to tell Mr Lambert that the house had been sold in order to help Patrick—and that was why she had been practically thrown out of the house that had been her home all her life.

'She's not very patient, she thinks he's seeking attention and has no sympathy. I can't see how they . . .'

'Maybe he felt you were leading too narrow a life and that it would do you good to go out into the world.'

'I doubt if he ever thought about me,' Megan said bitterly, then wished she hadn't been so honest as she saw Mr Lambert open his eyes wider as he stared at her.

'You could be wrong, of course,' Craig Lambert said slowly. 'Well, you had to find a job. I take it you told Mrs Arbuthnot and she told you I had already been there, asking if she could recommend someone. I know it seems strange, with a school like ours having to look for a dancing mistress, but I've set a very high standard for the staff and I wouldn't take just anyone. Often the girls have what used to be called "crushes" on the staff and I want to be

21

certain that the staff concerned will be a good influence on them. What I can't understand is why Mrs Arbuthnot, who obviously valued you highly and had no desire to lose you—why did she tell me about you? You've known her for some time?'

'All my life. She taught me all I know about dancing. She was a great dancer once, but broke her hip and it never got properly healed. I think she wanted me to get a job far away because she was afraid Aunt Lily would rope me in to look after them both . . .'

'And of course you'd have gone.'

Megan looked at him. 'I'd have had no choice, would I?' She laughed. 'Mrs Arbuthnot is a darling. She said that would be the end for me and my whole life would be ruined.'

'And you'd have had no chance to find a nice husband,' he said.

'I . . .' Megan looked at him again. 'I never thought of marriage. You see, I couldn't . . . well, I just couldn't leave Dad. He isn't so old, though his arthritis made him retire much earlier than he should have done and he could live for another thirty or forty years. The doctor says he's in fine health—'

'Apart from his arthritis.' There was a slightly sarcastic note in Craig Lambert's voice that annoyed Megan at once.

'It can be terribly painful,' she said quickly.

'I'm aware of that, Miss Crane,' he said. 'You seem to lay great stress on doing your

22

duty. Unusual in this day and age. Do you feel the same sense of duty as regards your brother?'

There was a long pause as she stared at him. What did he mean? What was he trying to trick her into saying?

'In a . . . in a way I suppose so, but I can't imagine Patrick ever needing me.'

Craig Lambert stood up. 'That's what you think,' he said. 'We'd better get going. I'll tell you more about the school on our way.'

Back in the spacious, luxurious car, Megan found it hard to concentrate on what Craig Lambert was saying, for she couldn't forget the way he had said: *That's what you think.* What had he meant? Was he planning to do some mean trick on Patrick and include her in it?

The car crawled along the winding narrow roads that wound up and down the mountains, into the deep valleys, then up far above it again. Megan sat meekly, trying to listen to what Craig Lambert was saying. She had her hands folded, but she had to dig her nails into the palms as she tried to force herself to concentrate.

'My grandfather had one son and three daughters. It was the girls he adored; he had no time for his son. Perhaps that was why my father . . .' Craig Lambert paused and then went on: 'My grandfather searched the world for a school good enough for the girls. He couldn't find one, so he built this one. Soon it

23

became famous, selective, and it had a long waiting list. When he died, my father took over.' His voice changed. 'Unfortunately he hadn't been properly trained to handle the responsibility of the job and soon it began to deteriorate and lose prestige. When he died, I came back from South America and had to repair the damage caused to the school and its name. I succeeded until a new problem arose. This island was far from the madding crowd, but suddenly it became a holiday centre. A number of people have come to live here whom we consider completely undesirable.' He looked at the girl sitting silently by his side and paused, as if giving her a chance to speak.

Megan said nothing. She felt it was wiser to hold her tongue, for she could feel the anger again. Why did he so condemn poor Patrick? All Patrick was doing was to earn a living, a living that wasn't made any easier by the extravagant girl he had married.

'Gradually, however,' Craig Lambert went on slowly, 'we're gradually erasing them.'

Megan had to cling her fingers together as anger swept through her. *Erase?* Could there be a more callous expression? In other words, wipe them out, force them to become bankrupt and lose everything just so that he could get rid of those he disliked?

'We have to have strict rules at the school,' Craig Lambert continued. 'There's always the danger of kidnapping to be faced, of course,

24

also of the wrong type of friends being made. These are not children we have at the school. Many of them are old enough to have been married several years, but their parents refuse to let them leave school because they feel they're safer here until a suitable husband can be found. This, as you can imagine, can cause some friction. No girl is allowed to move about the island alone. This is plainly understood.'

Poor things, Megan thought quickly. 'And the staff?' she asked, unable to resist saying it.

He showed no surprise or annoyance. 'That's quite different, of course. We only employ those we can trust, but we do ask them to always leave notice of where they go. This is to ensure that we can contact them immediately if they're needed.'

'What about transport?' Megan asked. 'The school seems an awful long way from the town.'

'Actually it isn't far. Perhaps I should say *unfortunately,* because I'd prefer us to be further away. However, we came this long way so that you could see something of the island and its beauty. Most of the staff have cars of their own. There are also buses on Wednesday and Sunday, going both ways. Naturally, when you want to visit your brother, we can arrange a lift.'

'Thank you . . .' Megan began, not sure if she liked the sound of that. Was Mr Lambert planning to keep her under observation when she visited Patrick? she wondered. 'Oh, look, isn't it gorgeous!' she cried impulsively, leaning forward as they passed a huge, aged tree whose trunk and branches were twined with the long clinging tendrils of a purple-flowered bougainvillea. 'What a marvellous colour!'

'What? Oh, yes, the bougainvillea. You know the name of the island we prefer? It has many names—ours is the Isle of Purple Flowers. Quite suitable.'

'It's all so beautiful.' Megan's voice was awed. Now they had left the mountains and were driving through what seemed like the avenues of trees they had passed earlier, then coming into the sunshine, passing by waterfalls that had looked like a silver line from the schooner but now were amazingly wide as the water frantically pushed its way through the rocks.

'We'll be there soon. Just round that cluster of trees. I hope you will find Miss Tucker congenial—our headmistress, a fine woman, but rather out of date in her view. Comes of a military family, hence very keen on discipline. As you can imagine, very few today can accept that, but here they must.'

Megan shivered. There had been something ominous in the way he had said *they must.* She could almost imagine him with a horsewhip in one hand . . . then she had to laugh. What an imagination she had! He couldn't be such a

26

monster or he wouldn't have been so friendly that day, going to the trouble of meeting her and bringing her this long way round . . .

She caught her breath. Or was it because he had wanted to question her? Had she unwittingly said something that could hurt Patrick? she wondered.

What would life at the school be like? she asked herself. It was beginning to sound like a prison. What he was implying was that you had to conform or get out! No wonder the salary was so generously high, and that once a year, return fares were paid to the staff so that they could go home for the long holiday. In addition Miss Wilmot had told her there was a flatlet for each member of the staff, who could cook for herself or go to the communal dining room as she preferred. Megan wondered which she would do. It rather depended on the other staff, she thought.

'Here we are,' Craig Lambert said, his voice proud, as the car left the trees and slowed up along the road leading up to Lambert School.

Megan gasped. She didn't know what she had expected to see, but it was certainly not this massive mansion built in the shape of an L, with courtyards, and two sides facing the sea. The chimneys were Elizabethan, long and decorated, the windows on the ground floor were large picture ones, but on the two floors above, the windows were smaller, but each room had a balcony. The garden in front was gay with flowers, everything symmetrically arranged so that nothing was out of place. On either side of the doorway stood a huge white-blossomed gardenia. On the other side of the building stretched tennis courts, hockey fields—she could even make out a distant golf course.

'Well?' Craig Lambert asked impatiently. 'You look surprised.'

She turned to stare at him. 'I didn't expect this. It's so English!'

'You sound disappointed. What's wrong with looking English?'

'Nothing, oh, nothing at all. It is beautiful, really marvellous,' she said quickly, and meant it.

It was just that it was the opposite of what she had expected, which was absurd anyhow. What had her foolish impossible dream to do with a school of this size? Yet she still felt disappointed. Had she come nearly seven thousand miles from England just to live in an English house?

'What a lovely lot of . . .' she began enthusiastically.

'Facilities for games? Yes, we watch our students' health carefully and always make sure they can play their part in a social world. Here we expect the staff to help and play *their* part. Now, Miss Crane,' Craig Lambert's voice changed, became grave and almost stern, 'I'm not always here. You must appreciate that

28

Miss Tucker is always in charge and conform to her wishes. Is that clear? The staff you may find difficult at first. It's inevitable in such a small confined community that adults of different nationalities will not always see eye to eye, but I must ask you to remain neutral as far as possible, since we have enough temperamental females here as it is.'

Megan coloured. Was that what he thought she was? A temperamental female?

'Not to worry,' he went on. 'I feel I know you well enough to trust you to soon adjust yourself, taking your part in the social life of the school as well as passing on your very excellent talent as a dancer. One final point.' His voice hardened. 'Please remember that you are on the *staff*. Do you understand? No nonsense about sympathising with the students. You're on the staff's side. Understand?'

A little puzzled, she nodded. The car was drawing nearer the huge house that seemed to tower above them almost ominously. Was she going to be happy here? she wondered. She glanced quickly at Craig Lambert. But he was staring proudly up at the school, no doubt delighting in the fact that he had made it become what his grandfather would have liked.

His school. Craig Lambert's school . . . that he was afraid some people were trying to destroy.

He turned to her. 'When we arrive, I must leave you at once. The servants will show you your flat. I'll send for you in about two hours' time—that'll give you time to wash and change before you meet Miss Tucker.' Even as he spoke, the car stopped. He was out of the car immediately, striding up the wide white steps into the door that had been opened.

Megan sat alone. Never had she felt so alone before.

A tall, slender dark-skinned girl came to the car.

'Would you this way please come?' she said politely, leading the way into the tall hall with its curving staircase and huge oil paintings on the walls.

Megan followed her up the stairs, down a long corridor, then the girl opened the door, stepped back and gave what might resemble a very mild curtsey.

'I hope it is all well,' the girl said. 'I am Odette. This is your flat.'

Slowly Megan walked in. First, there was a not-so-large but neither was it small, squarish room, brightly decorated with pale yellow walls, deep sea-green curtains that showed a wide open French door that led to a balcony. Megan was drawn immediately to the window and then stood there, hardly able to breathe, it was so beautiful.

She could look straight out over the garden to the Indian Ocean. How far away seemed the horizon, not a sign of a ship or even a fishing boat. When she turned, Odette had left her, so Megan explored on her own. The sitting-room had two armchairs, a desk, a small table and two chairs. Everything was very tidy and polished vigorously. The bedroom led out of the sitting-room and was narrow with a built-in wardrobe and a divan bed. Here again, the walls were pale yellow, the curtains and bedspread green. Out of the bedroom was a small bathroom with a shower and alongside it a tiny kitchen annexe, with a small electric cooker, refrigerator and dresser.

It was far nicer than she had dared to hope, Megan thought, as she wandered round. Her luggage was waiting for her. The air was hot but not too humid.

She began to unpack, frowning a little as she shook out the well-cut dresses of drip-dry material, some pale blue, others green or white. Miss Wilmot had taken her shopping. Part of the contract was that the school would supply what Craig Lambert called 'uniform'. Megan thought he had evidently been shocked by her drab clothes, and she had felt furious with him for suggesting that she couldn't buy her own clothes, or even choose them—but talking to Miss Wilmot had made Megan see it in a different light.

'The staff must set an example of perfect taste and good dressing,' Miss Wilmot had said gravely. 'They must be up to date but definitely not *avant-garde*.'

'How do the staff react? Or is it only me who's being treated like this?' Megan had asked, trying to hide her indignation.

Miss Wilmot's horrified expression had been answer enough.

'Of course not. I always advise the staff when they're first engaged. Certainly a few are difficult, but most of them will accept the common sense of it. They are allowed to wear what they like when they go off duty, but not if they are still in the school. Only if they go into the town, for instance. Even then, there are limits.'

'It sounds like a convent or a prison,' Megan had found herself saying. 'Do the staff really accept it.'

Miss Wilmot smiled coldly. 'They don't have to take the jobs, do they? It's up to them. The salaries are high, the perks even greater. The school has a name to keep up, we can't risk damaging it.'

Not that she should complain at all, Megan told herself, as she carefully hung up the clothes. Never in her life had she had such lovely well-cut dresses. There were even several evening dresses, for apparently the social life of the school was considered important. Miss Wilmot had shopped carefully, occasionally asking Megan if she *liked* the dress but more often consulting with the assistants and proving difficult to please.

Now, as Megan hastily showered and brushed her hair, twisting it round her head, leaving her slender neck exposed, she tried on a pale green dress. As she stared in the mirror at herself, she thought how grateful she should be. Never in her life had she dreamed of wearing a dress like this . . .

With her eyes watching the clock, because she mustn't be late on this first day, Megan tried to work out to whom she should be *grateful*. Miss Wilmot for choosing such attractive clothes? Craig Lambert for footing the bill? Mrs Arbuthnot for finding her the job? Perhaps her father for turning her out, Megan thought sadly, for it still hurt . . . or should the thanks go back still farther? To Patrick for needing money so urgently that it had triggered off the whole . . . whole incident, if it could be so called.

A gentle tap on the door made Megan jump. It was Odette.

'If *Mademoiselle* will follow me,' she said politely.

A little nervous, Megan obeyed. Craig Lambert's comments about the headmistress had not been exactly comforting: *a fine woman but rather out of date,* also Miss Tucker had come of a military family, hence *very keen on discipline.* He had even said he hoped she would be *congenial—so* it sounded as if he wasn't too sure they would be . . .

Odette led the way back downstairs, down

33

the lofty, cool hall to where it seemed to divide into various tributaries of corridors, leading away. She stopped outside a closed door, knocked, opened it and stood back.

'Mademoiselle Crane,' Odette said, then quietly left Megan and closed the door.

Megan stood just inside the room. She couldn't believe her eyes, for there was an almost monastic simplicity about the room that was in complete reverse to what she had seen, so far, of the rest of the school. Severe'y white walls, white curtains, a broad walnut desk with a chair behind it, and an armchair. A shadow of someone standing by the window moved.

He turned. It was Craig Lambert.

Looking her up and down, he nodded. 'Miss Wilmot has superb taste,' he said.

Flushing, Megan nodded. She couldn't speak, she was so angry. In other words, she hadn't superb taste? He was comparing her old-fashioned drab dress with this . . . this one that had cost probably twenty times as much as the dress Megan had worn and all she could afford.

'Miss Tucker won't be a moment. Sit down,' Craig Lambert said curtly.

The cosiest, most comfortable-looking item in the room was the armchair that Megan sank into, facing the desk.

'Well, how do you like your flat?' There was a note of impatience in Craig Lambert's voice.

Was it because she hadn't said a word so far? Megan wondered. Somehow she found her voice.

'It's lovely. It's really lovely,' she said.

He smiled. He smiled so rarely that it always startled her, for it completely altered his face. Normally it was so stern, almost as if carved in stone, but when he smiled, it was as if the skin, drawn taut over the bones, relaxed.

'I'm glad you like it. No regrets?' he asked, and then added: 'So far.'

'No, of course not,' Megan said quickly. Why was he always hinting that she was going to regret it, that it wouldn't all be roses and honey?

The door opened, Craig Lambert turned round promptly and Megan scrambled ungracefully to her feet.

Miss Tucker.

Megan saw a tall, thin woman dressed in a severely plain white jersey dress. She wore a crimson stone on a thin gold chain round her neck. She was not beautiful, yet in a way she had a fascinating face, for she had high cheekbones, and red hair. Really *red* hair, naturally red, Megan thought quickly, comparing it in her mind with Miss Wilmot's, which was obviously dyed.

'Welcome, Miss Crane.' Miss Tucker came forward, holding out her hand, shaking Megan's firmly, then releasing it. 'I'm sorry you had to wait. Do sit down,' she said, going behind the desk, then looking up at Craig Lambert.

'There's no need for you to be detained, Mr Lambert,' Miss Tucker said coldly. 'I think it would be wiser if we talked alone.'

He stood, feet apart, hands on his hips, and his eyes narrowed a little.

'I agree entirely, Miss Tucker, but first I want to make a few things clear if you have no objection.'

'Naturally I can have none,' Miss Tucker said, even more coldly. 'Would you care to sit down? I can get a chair.' Her hand was on the bell on the desk, but Craig Lambert put up his hand.

'Please don't bother, Miss Tucker. I shall only be here a few moments.'

'I see,' Miss Tucker replied, quite obviously showing by her tone of voice that she didn't, and had no intention of trying to *see*.

Megan, sitting silently, her hands moist with nervousness, was puzzled. Why this hostility between the headmistress and the owner of the school?

'Well?' Miss Tucker asked, the fingers of one hand drumming lightly on the desk.

Craig Lambert was not disturbed at all. He half-smiled before he began talking. 'In the first place, Miss Tucker, I must warn you that Miss Crane suffers from an outsize inferiority complex . . .'

Megan caught her breath, feeling the colour

36

surge through her cheeks. If they looked as red as they felt hot, she hated to think what she must look like. A boiled lobster, perhaps! How dared he! How could he be so cruel?

'She will, of course, deny this,' Craig Lambert continued, still looking with half-closed eyes at Megan. 'She's a fine dancer, one of the most natural I've ever seen. Unfortunately through her father's inability to move without help, Miss Crane had to leave school early after her 0-levels and also give up her dancing, which was, I consider, a great loss to the world.

'You may wonder, as she obviously does, why I went to a comparatively unknown school in Hastings to find a new dancing mistress. Actually I had been told by several people that the school had a good reputation. I must confess I'm rather tired of having entirely classical ballet dancing. I think dancing should interpret what the music means to you. Mrs Arbuthnot, who had instructed and then employed Miss Crane, allowed me to watch Miss Crane at work without her knowing it. As I think I've said, I was impressed. I liked the way she handled her pupils, too, and the way she behaved herself. I felt she would be an asset to the school.

'It's time we moved with the times.' He smiled again as if at himself. 'I think Miss Crane will satisfy us in every respect.' He stood straight, glancing down at his hands for a moment. 'I'm telling you this, Miss Tucker, because Miss Crane may come up against some hostility; it may be asserted that she's not fully qualified because she had not taken the usual examinations. I say it's time this was no longer considered necessary. I employed Miss Crane because I believe her to be an excellent dancer and teacher. I know that having asked you to support me in this, I can rely on you to give Miss Crane all the assistance required. That's all. Thank you.' He walked to the door and smiled at Megan. 'Don't look like a terrified rabbit, Miss Crane. I'm sure you'll be happy here and I know Miss Tucker will help you. I can rely on her,' he added, and left the room.

There was an uncomfortable silence as Megan stared at Miss Tucker. What had that all been about? she wondered unhappily. It was as if he had been cracking a whip, subtly threatening Miss Tucker . . . or, even worse, warning he would not tolerate any hostility shown towards Megan. Would there be hostility? Megan wondered anxiously.

'Mr Lambert is right, Miss Crane,' Miss Tucker said, her voice suddenly friendly. 'Don't look so frightened. I won't eat you.'

'I'm sorry.' Megan felt the bright colour again which made it all worse. 'I'm rather tired and . . . and Mr Lambert is right, I can't help wondering if I'm capable of doing . . . I mean, I wasn't trained as a teacher and . . .'

38

'If Mr Lambert has seen you dance and listened to your methods of teaching, you can rest assured, Miss Crane, that you *are* capable of coping.' Miss Tucker's face creased into a smile. 'Mr Lambert knows what he's talking about and is a good judge of character.'

'But why . . . what did he mean about . . . well . . .' Megan hesitated, looking for the right words. 'The hostility he talked of . . .'

'Well, that *is* rather difficult.' Miss Tucker stood up, moved to the window, drawing back the curtain a little so that both could see out of the window at the girls playing tennis. Miss Tucker turned round. 'Unfortunately Mr Lambert dismissed our last dancing mistress for no apparent reason. Quite abruptly, too. I'm aware that he made it worth her while to go, but there was no doubt about it, she didn't want to go. I'm afraid there's a feeling here that she was . . . well . . .'

'Erased?' Megan found herself saying, then wished she hadn't.

'Erased?' Miss Tucker repeated, a smile warming her face. 'A good word, and appropriate. I'm afraid the staff resent this, they feel Miss Pointer was sacked in order to give you the job.'

'But that's absurd! He didn't even know me.' Impulsively Megan was on her feet, going to join Miss Tucker at the window. 'When did he . . . when did Miss Pointer leave?'

'Six weeks ago.'

'Well, I wasn't looking for a job then,' Megan said. 'Please believe me, Miss Tucker. It all happened so quickly about three weeks ago . . .'

'Three weeks? Is that all? Suppose we sit down and you tell me just why you applied for the position, how you came to hear of it, and so on.' Miss Tucker's voice was kind so Megan went back to her chair quite happily.

'It all began when . . .' Megan stopped in time. She had been about to say *when Patrick wrote, saying he needed money urgently,* but instead she told Miss Tucker about the startling announcement made at the breakfast table.

'When my father said he wanted to sell the house and go and live with Aunt Lily, I felt awful,' Megan confessed. 'I had thought Dad needed me and suddenly I was a burden, a nuisance, in his way. I was very upset, and when Mrs Arbuthnot—I worked for her—saw me she made me tell her. I said I didn't know how I'd ever get a full-time job as I wasn't trained for anything, and then . . .'

'Then . . .?' Miss Tucker leaned forward over the desk, her face thoughtful.

'Then Mrs Arbuthnot told me that someone had visited her, asking if she could recommend anyone suitable for . . . for this job. Of course, believing I was tied down with Dad, she never thought of me and she had no one suitable and told him so, but this man—she didn't even

40

mention his name—gave her a phone number in case she ever should have someone suitable.'

'So your Mrs Arbuthnot phoned him and he came to watch you, unseen by yourself? And then, I imagine, interviewed you?'

'Yes. I was amazed, but,' Megan smiled, 'it was the answer to my prayer, because I was feeling desperate.'

'It hasn't taken long for you to get here?'

'No. That was one of the conditions—that I had to come out at once. I couldn't leave Dad, so we sorted out everything, sold our furniture, though Dad took quite a lot down to Dorset— that's where Aunt Lily lives—and the house is up for sale. Dad went straight down to Dorset as soon as he could and Miss Wilmot . . .'

'Supervised the purchase of your wardrobe,' Miss Tucker said dryly. 'Did you mind?'

Megan bit her lip. 'In a way, yes. In another way, no. I've never been able to afford such clothes. I was angry at first, I thought it was . . . well, suggesting I couldn't afford to buy good clothes or had any good sense, but Miss Wilmot made everything plain.'

'She would,' Miss Tucker said dryly. That was another surprise to Megan. So Miss Tucker didn't like Miss Wilmot either? 'It must have been chaotic—with the house to clear up, clothes to buy, a passport to get, for I imagine you hadn't one, the necessary injections.'

41

'It was,' Megan agreed with a smile. 'I still don't seem to know quite where I am. It's all happened so fast.'

'And it wasn't, then, until three weeks ago that you knew you needed a job?'

'Yes. It was quite a few days before I met Mr Lambert. I was so surprised when he engaged me. I mean, I've not been trained.'

'Miss Crane,' Miss Tucker's voice had become cold and stern, 'I don't wish to hear you say those words again. Mrs Arbuthnot obviously trained you satisfactorily or she would neither be employing you nor would she have recommended you to Mr Lambert. That point is settled. You may not have passed the usual examinations, but you are suitably trained. Is that understood?'

'Yes, Miss Tucker,' startled by the change in the headmistress's voice, Megan said the words meekly.

'Secondly, you must not allow any malicious gossip or even teasing to affect you in any way. Some of our staff have a peculiar sense of humour and you may find yourself called the teacher's pet.'

'*The teacher's pet?*' Megan echoed, shocked.

Miss Tucker let herself smile. 'They can be very childish, the staff, and also easily jealous. We must make it plain to them that your being employed here has nothing to do with the dismissal of Miss Pointer. There must be some reason for doing that. I think Mr Lambert

42

should have consulted the Board before doing anything so drastic. But there is, of course, another side to it. Miss Pointer was always rather a rebel, not willing to conform happily with our way of living, so it's quite possible that she did something that we couldn't tolerate. Mr Lambert would keep it quiet to save her being hurt. He has such a soft heart,' Miss Tucker added, a little contemptuously.

A soft heart, Megan thought, unable to believe it. How could Craig Lambert have a soft heart and be doing his best to ruin poor Patrick?

'Well, now.' Miss Tucker drew out some sheets of typed notes from the drawer of the desk. 'I'll give you these to read. It's a list of the classes you will teach, the rooms they will be in, the names of those who will play the piano for you. You will see it's a pretty heavy programme, but I feel certain you can cope. As your hours are long, you will be left out of intracurricular tasks, but I would like you to join in our social life. Certain nights of the week, we play bridge, for instance. You can play?'

'I'm afraid I can't.'

'How tiresome. Well, you can join the evening classes with the girls. Mr Parr will teach you. Mr Parr . . .' Miss Tucker added, frowning thoughtfully. 'Not always an easy man to work with, unfortunately. He's an artist, certain he's no good.' Miss Tucker smiled. 'How hard it is to convince people who lack self-confidence! I often wonder why they don't trust themselves to be able to do anything they tackle.'

'Perhaps . . . perhaps no one has told them they can,' Megan began.

Miss Tucker nodded. 'You could be right, I suppose. When one is young, one needs a certain amount of praise. You got none?'

'No.'

'There are many of you in the family?'

'Just two of us. Patrick . . .' Megan stopped dead. Now why, she asked herself miserably, had she to bring in Patrick, when she saw the way Miss Tucker's face had changed.

'Not *the* Patrick Crane?' Miss Tucker sounded shocked.

Megan's cheeks flamed. 'He lives on the island,' she said defiantly.

'Does Mr Lambert know?' Miss Tucker literally demanded.

'Of course,' Megan told her. 'Naturally I told him I had a brother living here. It seemed such a coincidence.'

'It certainly does . . .' Miss Tucker seemed to relax in her chair, folding her fingers together, not looking at Megan. 'A most strange coincidence. Now, where was I? Oh, yes, Miss Weston will be able to advise you as to where the different rooms are. She's in the flat next to you. You are used to dealing with children?'

'Yes, and . . . and adults,' said Megan.

Miss Tucker smiled, an oddly cynical smile. 'Adults! I'm afraid you'll find some very strange girls here. Now, tonight is our social night. Please wear an evening dress. We all mix together and dance. Dinner is served at eight o'clock, but I'll tell Miss Weston to take you down. That's all, thank you.'

Megan stood up. 'Thank you, Miss Tucker.' She glanced at her watch. It was four hours to dinner time. 'Is there anything I should do?'

'No, Miss Crane. You start work tomorrow. Why not wander around? Get to know the school. Most of the classes are over by now and the girls will be outside, playing games. There's plenty to watch.'

'Yes, I'm sure, thank you, Miss Tucker.' Megan almost ran to the door, eager to be outside. Miss Tucker, despite her superficial friendliness, was rather terrifying in many ways. Now Megan could understand Craig Lambert's remarks about Miss Tucker's military family. Megan could almost hear Miss Tucker's huge, furious voice shouting out commands.

As she closed the door, she jumped. Craig Lambert was waiting in the hall. He came to meet her.

'She took a long time! Come along, I'm going to show you round,' he said.

But should he? Megan was wondering. If she was already being called *teacher's pet,*

45

wouldn't it make things worse if she was seen being shown round by him?

'Perhaps we . . . I mean, it might be . . .' she began, stumbling over the words.

Maybe Craig Lambert understood what she was trying to say. He took her arm firmly in his hand.

'Of course we should,' he said. 'It was not a request I made, but a command I gave.'

Looking up at him, startled, she saw the impatient anger in his eyes and she shivered. What had she let herself in for? she was asking herself, as they walked down the endless corridors, pausing by the empty rooms which were huge in many cases.

It was a very fine school, Megan thought, and yet somehow so different from an ordinary school. She could hear the shouts and laughter from outside where the girls of all ages were playing games. From behind some closed doors, came the sound of music or the chatter of girls arguing but they met no one at all. It was as if the school had been deserted. She listened as Craig Lambert talked; he was interesting, his views on education fascinated her, there was no doubt he was determined the school should be a good one in every respect.

But equally obvious, she thought with a shiver, that he was determined to keep it that way. No matter what it cost.

CHAPTER II

That first evening was rather a nightmare for Megan, for she felt absolutely exhausted and everything, even a smile, was an effort. She couldn't explain her feelings; she wasn't actually tired, yet the ability to *do* anything, to say anything, or even to think sensibly, seemed to have left her and she felt as if all her life had been squeezed out of her.

Craig Lambert escorted her all over the huge building, and this alone was tiring, for he strode ahead, talking over his shoulder, making it hard for her to hear what he said and to give intelligent answers. He showed her the laboratories, the gymnasium, the girls' sleeping quarters, their play rooms, the senior girls' own sitting-rooms, the staff's common room. It was impressive, but Megan was too tired to appreciate it.

Later, when she escaped from him, she took refuge in a deep, warm bath, trying to relax, but her brain refused to slow down as inside her head it whirled her anxious thoughts.

Could it all have happened by chance, she asked herself, or was it far too much of a coincidence? Had Craig Lambert employed the sister of a man he was determined to wipe out—financially, not physically, she thought hastily, though it was physically in a way, for

47

Mr Lambert would obviously like Patrick to leave the island!

Was it purely by chance that the sister of the man Mr Lambert wanted to *erase* had been given this job?

After all, it could so easily not have happened, though, she thought, as she turned on the hot water tap again, loving the feel of the water against her skin, feeling for the moment safe, for she had not got to keep tense, watching her every word, waiting for one of Mr Lambert's suddenly-thrown-at-her questions which always found her off guard.

Now look at it sensibly, she told herself. Nothing could have happened if Patrick hadn't written that desperate letter, asking for money. Nor could it have happened had her father not already discussed with Aunt Lily the sharing of her cottage in Dorset. In addition to this, Miss Pointer had been teaching here, so how could Mr Lambert have known she was going to leave?

Megan caught her breath. But it was Mr Lambert who had sacked Miss Pointer. How could he have known Miss Pointer would do something that deserved dismissal? Perhaps she hadn't? Perhaps he had just got rid of her in order to give Patrick's sister the job? But there again, Megan thought, she came up against a lot of contradictions. The time element, for one thing. How could Mr Lambert have known *when* Patrick was writing

48

to his father? How could Mr Lambert have known Megan would ask for Mrs Arbuthnot's help? Indeed, *how* could Mr Lambert have even known that Patrick's sister lived in Hastings and worked for Mrs Arbuthnot? None of that made sense, Megan told herself, as she stood up, dripping with water, and wrapped the towel round her body.

Of course, she went on thinking, there were other things that didn't make sense. For one, how was it Mr Lambert knew so much about her? Small things, yet things she felt sure she hadn't told him herself? Of course it might have been Mrs Arbuthnot, for she was fond of talking.

She looked at her watch. Comfortably off for time, she saw. She went to the window. How dark it was! A thin slice of the moon shone bravely in the sky. She could hear the roar of the ocean as it pounded against the rocks,

She dressed carefully, choosing a pale green dress, long, high-necked but sleeveless. Her hair she had swept up from her face, pinning it carefully, allowing only two curls to fall on her cheeks. She looked at her reflection in the long mirror carefully. She wanted to make a good impression, this first night, particularly. She was twenty, but she was always being told how much younger she looked. Carefully she made up, using the false eyelashes that Miss Wilmot had shown her so patiently how to use.

'It is essential,' Miss Wilmot said, 'that you take care not only of your deportment and behaviour but your appearance. It is so easy for a rebellious teenage girl to make herself look a mess as part of her defiance. This we will not tolerate.'

Megan had wondered how they kept the girls at school, for how many today would tolerate such treatment? She thought how interesting in many ways it would be to meet the girls and find out what kind they were.

There was a knock on her door and even as she spoke, it opened. A tall girl stood there. One of the staff? Megan wondered. She looked young, too.

'Miss Crane? I'm Petronella Weston. I think Miss Tucker told you about me?'

'Of course. Please come in,' Megan said eagerly.

Petronella Weston was tall, slender and had very dark hair and matching eyes. Her voice was husky and friendly in an impersonal way.

'Well, what do you think of the convent?' she asked with a smile.

'It's very impressive.'

Miss Weston gave a little snort. 'It's supposed to be.'

'It seems very strict. I mean for this day and age.'

Laughing a little, Miss Weston sat down. 'But we get paid well. Isn't that right? We don't have to stay.'

Megan nodded. 'Very right.'

'How do you get on with Miss Tucker?' Hesitating a little, Megan said: 'Not too badly, but she was a bit . . well . . .'

Miss Weston laughed. 'How right you are! A very good description. *A bit . . . well . . .* She can be quite a dragon, but she does a good job. Trouble is that she and Craig Lambert rarely see eye to eye. By the way, what do you think of him?'

'Think of him?' Megan's mouth was dry. She must be careful what she said. 'Well, I hardly know him. I'd only met him once before today.'

'Once?' Miss Weston sounded startled. 'He engaged you after meeting you once?'

Megan, perched on the edge of a chair, smiled. 'Well, he saw me twice before, but I didn't know he was there.'

'I don't get it.'

'I know, but . . . well, it sounds funny, but . . .but Mrs Arbuthnot—I taught at her dancing college—knew I was nervous, so maybe it was her idea.'

'Sounds more like his,' Petronella Weston said drily. 'Go on.'

'Well, there's not much to say. Apparently he watched me take two classes without my knowing he was there. Mrs Arbuthnot has always had . . .'

'I know, one of those *windows.*' Miss Weston sounded impatient. 'Then you met him and he

51

asked questions. Right?'

'Right,' Megan laughed. 'Did he do it to you?'

'He does it to us all. I think he must have a sadistic streak in him because he seems to delight in cutting one down to size. Has he done that to you yet?' Petronella Weston's dark eyes were narrowed as she looked at Megan's face.

Megan was thinking fast. Had Mr Lambert ever made her feel small? 'No, actually he hasn't . . . oh yes, he did, but then I found it happened to everyone.'

'What happened to everyone?'

'Miss Wilmot choosing my clothes. I felt . . . well, I thought Mr Lambert was implying that I couldn't afford to buy decent clothes . . . which, actually, I couldn't!' Megan laughed. 'And also implying my lack of taste, but I gather Miss Wilmot is always given the task?'

Petronella Weston laughed. 'Usually she has fights with us. I imagine you were more biddable. We'd better go down—mustn't make you late on your first night. Miss Tucker is a maniac about punctuality—so is Craig Lambert, for that matter.'

Outside the flat, there seemed a lot of people. Men, older women and girls, all swirling round, going down the curving staircase, laughter and voices filling the air. Megan found herself being introduced to so many people that she gave up the vain attempt

52

to remember faces and link them with names. At dinner she sat next to a silent man with dark hair and a thin mouth. His name was Paul Taft. On the other side was a girl whose long, black hair fell almost to her waist. She had a rebellious, sulky mouth. Her name, she said, was Anarita.

'You're going to teach us to dance?'

Megan smiled. 'Yes.'

'Why did Miss Pointer go?' Anarita asked.

Megan's heart seemed to sink. Oh no! Were the pupils also involved in it? The silent man on Megan's other side looked coldly at the girl.

'She broke one of the school's rules so she had to go,' he said sternly, and then looked away.

'Rules!' Anarita almost snarled the words. She looked at Megan. 'How old are you?'

The man turned round again. 'That is a question ladies do not ask, Anarita.'

'But I'm not a lady,' Anarita said, tossing back her hair.

'Obviously not,' he said drily. 'Though we're trying to make you one.' He turned away again.

Megan felt uncomfortable. A sort of fight was going on across her.

'You liked Miss Pointer?' she asked.

Anarita shrugged. 'She was all right, I suppose. A bit of a bore. I hope your teaching methods are more interesting.'

At last the dinner, which had been very

good, was over and everyone was supposed to mix. The hall where dancing was held seemed crowded and might have been any ordinary party, Megan thought, but for the main difference, which was too few men! Megan found herself dancing with all the male staff in turn. Some she liked, some made her feel uncomfortable as they kept asking her how she had heard of the job, Obviously they all felt strongly about Miss Pointer's dismissal and it was not helping Megan to be welcomed. Finally, feeling tired and bewildered, she found somewhere to sit out of sight, on a stone bench, half-hidden under the stairs by curtains. But as she sat down, she found she wasn't alone, for a man sat there. He scrambled to his feet with some difficulty.

'Miss Crane, I imagine?' he said, holding out his hand.

Megan shook his, grateful for the friendly gesture. She couldn't see him very plainly, but there wasn't much to see. He was the type of man no one could describe with his pale brown hair, a pale skin and freckles on his nose.

'I'm Frank Parr,' he said. 'Won't you sit down?'

Megan obeyed. 'Thanks. I've heard of you. You've got to teach me bridge.'

He pretended to groan. 'Heaven help us both, because I'm an appalling teacher!'

'And I shall be an appalling pupil?' Megan laughed again. She suddenly felt relaxed, no

54

longer afraid.

'I'll soon see to that,' Frank Parr smiled. 'You're much younger than we expected.'

'I'm twenty.'

He grinned. 'I'm twenty-eight, so you seem quite a kid. Think you're going to be happy here? By the way, is it true you're Patrick Crane's sister?'

Taken aback, for it was a question she hadn't expected, Megan stared at him.

'Well, yes, I am,' she said defiantly, her body stiffening.

'No business of ours,' he said as if reading her thoughts. 'It just makes it all rather surprising.'

'It does?' Megan drew a deep breath. 'What makes what surprising?' she asked.

Frank Parr turned to look at her. 'If you don't know, maybe I'd better not tell you.'

Megan twisted her fingers together, gazing down at them. 'Well, I rather gather Mr Lambert doesn't approve of my brother.'

'Understatement of the year. That's why it's so odd that he should have engaged a member of the Crane family. Did he know you were Patrick's sister?'

'I don't think so. When I told him, he seemed surprised and rather . . .'

'Shocked?' Frank Parr chuckled. 'If he didn't know, I bet he was. How do you get on with your brother?'

'I haven't seen him for three years. Not

since he got married and came out here.'

'What does he think of you coming out here?'

'I don't know.'

Frank Parr chuckled. 'It must have been a shock to him. His sister on the other side of the river! The acceptable side, of course. Have you met Gaston Duval?'

'No, I haven't. You're the second one who's asked me that.' Megan was getting a bit annoyed with all the questions.

'I bet I know who was the first. Craig Lambert. Right?'

Her cheeks were red, much to her annoyance. 'Yes, he did. So what?'

Frank Parr chuckled. 'So what? Nothing. Just my cheeky inquisitiveness. Sorry, Miss Crane. Now seriously, how come you're here sitting talking to me when you should be dancing?'

'I was dancing, but . . .'

'No one very enticing, eh?' Frank Parr chuckled. 'Wouldn't do to have handsome men on the staff. Bad enough the girls' crushes as it is. Just think, they have crushes on me!' he laughed.

'And why not?' Megan asked, her eyes demure.

He chuckled. 'You don't fool me, girl. I know I'm one of those men who might just as well not exist.'

Megan remembered what Miss Tucker had

56

said: that Frank Parr had an outsize inferiority complex.

'And what's wrong with you?' Megan asked. 'I've enjoyed talking to you.'

'Mademoiselle, you are so sweet . . .' Frank Parr said dramatically, lifting Megan's hand and kissing it.

At the same moment the curtain was jerked back and Craig Lambert stood there.

'I've been looking for you, Miss Crane,' he said accusingly.

Megan and Frank Parr both stood, Frank obviously having a little trouble to get up.

'I was tired,' Megan began.

'Can you blame her?' Frank Parr joined in. 'The miles she's flown, the new life, leaving her father . . . I bet you miss him, Miss Crane . . .'

Megan felt her eyes fill with tears. Perhaps that was why she felt so alone. All her life her father had been there, needing her, yet being someone she could turn to at any time. And now there was no one. No one she could trust.

'Yes, she must be tired,' Craig Lambert said curtly. 'Just one dance with me, Miss Crane, and then off to bed.'

Megan hesitated. She had no desire to dance with this man she couldn't trust, yet . . . Like all the things he said to her, it hadn't been a request but a command.

'Thank you, Mr Lambert,' she said demurely, but as she said goodnight to Frank

Parr, he winked at her.

On the floor, in Craig Lambert's arms, Megan felt everyone must be staring at her, and talking about her, she thought unhappily. Was Mr Lambert making the situation any easier for her by insisting on dancing with her?

All the same he danced well and in a few moments she lost the tension she felt and relaxed, delighted without realising it at the way he led her, his long legs covering the ground with surprising speed. As the music came to an end, he smiled at her—one of his rare smiles which made them more noticeable.

'You're a good dancer,' he said.

She was so relaxed she could be honest. 'I was just going to say the same to you. I enjoyed it.'

'I'm glad,' he told her, and led her off the dance floor. 'Now, time for bed.'

'Should I say goodnight to Miss Tucker?' Megan, conscious of the eyes on them, asked nervously.

'I'll explain,' he said, and led the way to the central hall with the beautiful curving staircase.

They were silent as he escorted her to the door of her flat. Megan felt ill at ease, wondering if she should talk ; wondering, too, if he always escorted the staff to their flats?

He waited as she fumbled in her small diamanté-trimmed handbag; he waited until she had opened the door and turned to say

58

goodnight. Then he frowned.

'It's not very wise, Miss Crane, on your first night here to sit alone with one of the staff. Already the girls are talking about you, because you're the youngest and most attractive member of the staff, but surely for your first night . . .'

'I didn't know he was there. I was tired and found the seat . . .'

'I see,' Craig Lambert said, but she knew he didn't. Nor did he believe her. 'Frank Parr has been with us for some time. He's a brilliant artist, gifted with the art of passing it on to others. Hitherto he has been without any blemish on his character.'

Megan's cheeks were flaming red; she was so angry, she felt herself shaking. Are you suggesting I was trying to seduce . . .'

Craig Lambert chuckled. 'Hardly, Miss Crane. You're not the type. Unfortunately Frank Parr has a sentimental heart and you might . . . well, I'm just warning you, Miss Crane, we do not tolerate affairs among the staff. I would advise you to avoid being seen alone with Mr Parr in future.'

'But that's absurd,' Megan said angrily. 'He was the only really friendly one. I'm not going to snub him simply because . . .'

'You aren't?' Craig Lambert's voice rose slightly. She stared at him and struggled to regain control of her temper.

'Please believe me, Mr Lambert,' she said,

59

her voice still uneven. 'Mr Parr was not making passes at me, nor is he the sort of man to do so.'

'Why was he kissing your hand?' Craig Lambert demanded.

Megan could laugh. 'It was a joke. Miss Tucker told me he had an outsize inferiority complex.' She paused for a moment, wondering if she should tackle him about saying *she* had such a complex, but decided not to at the time. It could wait!' Then he said some of the girls had crushes on him and he said he couldn't understand it as he was the sort of man who might just as well not exist. I remembered what Miss Tucker had said, so I treated it as a joke and asked him what was wrong with him and that I'd enjoyed our talk. Which was true,' she added defiantly, 'because he was the most friendly one of all I've met tonight. So he said something like *Mademoiselle, you are so sweet* and kissed my hand. It was just . . . well, one of those things It didn't mean anything to either of us.'

'I see,' Craig Lambert said slowly, but she knew he was not believing a word she had said. 'So long as you're both aware that it meant nothing. You are, however, very young and Parr is a romantic. We can't afford to lose our dancing teacher as soon as she arrives.' He turned away, but she acted without thought, clutching him by the arm.

'Mr Lambert, why did you sack Miss

60

Pointer?' she asked.

He turned back and looked at her. His face changed, it was just as she had seen it before, as if it was made of stone.

'That,' he said, 'is my business. Goodnight.'

CHAPTER III

Megan's first few days at the Lambert School were not too happy, but her real shock was to come on the fourth day.

When she awoke the morning after the social evening, she went and stood by the window, drinking in the beauties of the deep blue sea and the foam-tossed waves, and then she shivered. How was the job going to turn out? She felt she had so many enemies, which was perhaps rather absurd, but Frankie Parr had been the only really friendly one.

She washed and dressed quickly, choosing a rather demure pale blue dress, and went down to the dining room. The girls were all sitting at their tables and the roar of voices hit her as she walked in. She stood still for a moment, looking round, then she heard a soft whistle. Looking in that direction, she saw Frank Parr, beckoning to her from where he sat at what was, obviously, the staff table.

Sitting by him, as he talked and joked, she found some of her nervousness go. Several other members smiled and spoke to her, but it was Frank who seemed to have taken her under his wing.

'Did the old devil tick you off for sitting alone with me?' Frank Parr asked Megan suddenly.

Her red cheeks made it impossible for her to deny it. 'In a sense, yes, but when I explained . . .'

'He said he understood. Right? I suppose he warned you to keep away from me?' Frank Parr's eyes were amused as he watched her tell-tale cheeks. 'I know. I'm the Don Juan of the college.' He made a dramatic movement of his hand going across his heart, and Paul Taft, sitting opposite, frowned.

'It's hardly fair to Miss Crane to attract attention, Parr,' he said curtly.

Megan remembered Paul Taft from the dinner the night before. He had been so quiet until he scolded the girl.

Frank Parr laughed. 'How can she avoid attracting interest, Taft old boy, when she's such a choice dish?'

'Really, Parr!' Paul Taft looked disgusted and then turned to Megan. 'Please forgive my friend for his brashness. I trust that you will be happy with us.' He spoke with almost pedantic politeness, yet Megan found herself liking him.

'I understand, Mr Taft,' she said with a smile. 'Don't worry, I won't take Mr Parr seriously.'

'Oh, woe is me, alack, alas!' Frank Parr pre-

62

tended to groan. 'She's seen through me already. I have no hopes!'

It was the same all through the meal, with Frank joking and making Megan laugh, and even dour-faced Mr Taft's mouth kept quivering as if he was trying not to smile.

After that, Megan consulted her rota lists and made her way in search of the right room and her pupils. It turned out to be far easier than she had expected. Indeed, the actual teaching was the easiest part of her life those first days. The pianists, generally elderly men, were charming and really gallant, playing well and with feeling. The girls, chatting away until she stopped them, seemed to be eager to try her new ideas of dancing.

Perhaps it was the meals that were the biggest trial. Megan would go and join the staff at their table, hoping she might find an empty seat by Frank Parr. Usually she did, and then it was all right, but if she sat next to another member, a 'stranger' really even though they had been introduced, it was rather an ordeal, for the questions came pounding at her like the waves against rocks.

'Weren't you lucky to get this job?'

'I imagine you have some relation who knows the Lamberts?'

'What made you come out here—wouldn't life in London be more fun?'

'How long have you known Craig Lambert?'

The last question was the one most used

and Megan began to get tired of constantly saying she had only met him once and that was three weeks before. She often wondered how much Miss Tucker had told them, but no one mentioned Miss Pointer, the dancing mistress, who had been sacked for some unknown reason and Megan Crane swiftly moved in to take her place.

All the same it worried Megan, though she couldn't see that any of it was her fault. Perhaps Craig Lambert had been displeased with Miss Pointer for some time and had therefore made enquiries for her replacement? That would explain a lot of things.

That evening she had her first bridge lesson. There were quite a few other pupils, mostly girls over fifteen, and with Frank Parr's jokes, it was rather hilarious. There was probably more laughter than learning, Megan thought once when she glanced up thinking she had seen Craig Lambert glancing in the doorway, but did that really matter? They would all learn bridge more easily if they enjoyed doing it.

Oddly enough, apart from that quick glimpse which might, she thought, have been her imagination, Megan didn't see Craig Lambert until the fourth day. By then she had begun to settle down, had made several friends among the staff, and of course, there was always Frank.

She had just finished a class and was wearing her leotard as they had been doing modern dancing and she had demonstrated the way it should be done while Mr Anstruther, the elderly pianist, had clapped impulsively when she finished so the girls had joined in. Afterwards Mr Anstruther, his white hair slightly ruffled, for he had a knack of running his hands through it when he came to the end of whatever he was playing, said:

'You are too good a dancer to be teaching, Miss Crane.' He spoke gravely as he collected his music together.

Megan had flushed happily. 'Thank you,' she had said.

'It was a pity you had to stop training, but blood is thicker than water, isn't it?' Mr Anstruther said, then sighed. 'What a lucky man your father was to have a daughter like you!'

The girls had streamed out of the room and Megan gave it one quick look round, for things were apt to be left behind and it was easier to trace their owners if the class concerned was known. So it came about that she left the room alone and was startled to find Craig Lambert waiting in the corridor.

'Miss Crane,' he asked in that authoritative, snapping manner, 'could I have a word with you?'

'Of course,' she said. Wondering what she had done wrong this time, Megan followed

65

him to a small room lined with books. Just inside the door Craig Lambert stood on one side, letting her go through ahead, then closing the door.

'I'm going into town this afternoon and I see you are free, so I wondered if I could give you a lift, Miss Crane? I'm sure you're eager to see your brother. You've heard from him?'

The sun was making the sea glitter like a million diamonds, Megan saw, as she stared out of the window, taking a deep breath, for she must be on her guard now, and careful of what she said.

'No,' she answered with equal curtness, for it was no business of Craig Lambert's.

'You mean to say he hasn't written or telephoned? Surely a brother . . .' There was the amused sarcastic note she hated in Craig Lambert's voice.

'I don't think he knows I'm here,' she said. 'Unless my father wrote and told him.'

'But surely you want to see him? Your own brother?' The sarcasm was growing more intense and Megan's nails dug deeper into the palms of her hands as she controlled her temper. 'Or Georgina, his very beautiful wife. Aren't you good friends with her, either?'

Megan could feel the colour in her cheeks. 'Georgina and I were never friends. I hardly knew her when she married Patrick and they went abroad almost immediately.'

'I see. A very strange relationship. I would

66

have thought you would be eager to meet them. Anyhow, I'll take you in this afternoon. Meet me at the front at two-fifteen,' he finished quickly, turning, opening the door and waiting for her to go out.

It was a ruthless brush-off, Megan thought as she hesitated. What should she do? she asked herself. Tell him the truth: that she had no desire to see either Patrick or Georgina, or would he immediately think she was involved with them? She just didn't know what to do. Or if she went, would he go with her? Using her as an instrument to *erase* Patrick? Yet how could she be used in such a way? Surely she was exaggerating the whole thing?

So she nodded. 'Thank you, Mr Lambert,' she said politely, and left the room.

As the door closed behind her, she sighed. If she had had any idea there was to be so many complications, she would have refused the job. She had no desire to hurt Patrick— after all, he was her brother, and as nice old Mr Anstruther had said, blood was thicker than water!

She dressed carefully after lunch, choosing a leaf-green silk suit, carefully making up, wondering if Patrick would recognise her. Three years ago, she had been little more than a schoolgirl. Now . . .? She frowned at her reflection: if only she didn't look so young, she thought.

The white Rolls was waiting for her. Craig

Lambert walked out of the front door just behind her.

'Full marks,' he said. 'Punctual to the second.'

She glanced at him quickly, but could see no smile. So he wasn't joking? Who did he think he was, anyhow? she asked herself. A sergeant-major?

The road went along the coast, with the palm trees bending against the wind and the little sandy coves most inviting on this hot day. It was a much shorter way than the one they had driven when she arrived and she remembered that Craig Lambert had said he had wanted to show her the beauties of the island. Very thoughtful of him, and, considering his behaviour over other things, rather surprising.

They drove through the small town, along the wharf, past the jetty. No schooner was in, so there were few people on it, but still people crowded the pavements by the shops, and the cars and cycles seemed to be having a perpetual fight. Past the town, everything changed. It lost the tropical old-world look that had delighted Megan and suddenly became almost American in its modernisation.

The tall pencil-like hotel soared up into the sky, the grass before it was scattered with brightly-covered sunshades tilted over tables. Along the front were all sorts of enticements for the tourists' children. Donkey rides; a pool with self-piloted small boats; small zoos with monkeys and snakes apparently their main attraction.

'It seems so unlike the other side of the island,' Megan said, so surprised she forgot to watch what she said, as she had warned herself to do earlier.

'Naturally,' Craig Lambert said, his voice bitter. 'This is not my land.'

She turned to look at him. 'The rest is?'

'Yes. Seven-tenths of this island is mine, but the rest is not. Surely you've heard of the Lambert Folly?' When she shook her head, he went on: 'As you know my grandfather bought the island and built the school. Unfortunately my father was a different kind of man. A gambler . . .' He paused, and repeated the word as if it left a nasty taste in his mouth. 'A gambler. He gambled with the land as his money. Always there have been people after the island, seeing it as a good tourist centre. I bought back most of what my father had sold . . . but I haven't got it all back,' he said, almost sadly, Megan noticed, and then he added: 'yet.'

There was a strangely disturbing threat about the way he said *yet*, a vicious ruthlessness, she thought. In other words, no holds barred, but he was going to get back the whole island!

Now the car was pulling up before a single-storied building with large curtained windows and above the door, the notice:

69

'CRANE DANCING STUDIO'

On the other side was a very modern single-storied house with an enormous picture window and a garden, bright with vividly red, yellow and blue flowers and two palm trees, moving gently in the wind.

The chauffeur opened the door of the car and Megan got out. Her hands felt damp. How was Patrick going to take this? she wondered worriedly. Maybe—and this thought had not struck her before—maybe he would see her as Craig Lambert's accomplice . . . or he might even think she had come out to see if he was telling the truth and really needed the money he asked for. It seemed to her that no matter what she did, she would always be suspected.

To her dismay, she found Craig Lambert walking with her to the front door. She rang a heavy bell whose carved handle jangled as she pulled it.

'I'll fetch you at five o'clock,' Craig Lambert was saying, turning away as he spoke, just as the door opened.

Megan stared at the man standing there. Three years since she had last seen him. Now he looked taller, was much thinner, his blond hair cut in a modern style, huge circles of sunglasses hiding his expression.

He frowned, looking puzzled. 'Can I . . .'

Megan's eyes stung suddenly. He didn't even know her!

'Patrick, it's me, Megan. Don't you remember me?'

His surprise was evident. It was as if seeing her had jolted him, because, for a moment, his mouth sagged open and it was obvious he found it difficult to greet her normally.

'Why, Megan, this is a surprise!' he exclaimed, and the words suddenly died, as if sliced, for he saw Craig Lambert, standing there, looking at them both thoughtfully. 'What on . . .' Patrick began to say, his voice harsh, but Craig Lambert lifted his hand.

'I'll fetch you at five o'clock, Miss Crane,' he said and, turning, walked to the waiting car.

Patrick stared at him and then turned to Megan. 'What the devil are you doing out here?' he asked, sounding annoyed. 'And how did you get mixed up with that . . . that . . .' Then he seemed to realise that Craig Lambert must be able to see them, so he stepped back. 'You'd better come in,' he told Megan.

The hall was lofty and cool. Georgina came running out of a room. She was even more beautiful than Megan had remembered—tall, slim, dark hair piled high on her head, dark eyes, a full rather sulky mouth.

'What's that man doing here?' Georgina asked angrily, then stopped dead. She had obviously not seen Megan, who must have been just out of sight of the window. 'Megan? What on earth . . ?'

'That's what I want to know,' Patrick said

71

angrily. 'Come in and sit down. Just why are you here?' he demanded.

It was hardly the welcome of a sister he hadn't seen for several years, Megan thought, glad that Craig Lambert was not there to make a sarcastic comment. She looked round while Georgina rang a little silver bell and told the Creole servant when she came to bring in the ice.

'We must have a drink to welcome you here, Megan,' Georgina said almost cheerfully, frowning at Patrick who was standing glowering down at Megan. Patrick was wearing a smart silk smoking jacket, Megan noticed, and wearing white trousers. He didn't look desperately poor, she thought. Nor did Georgina in her lush red silk trouser suit.

'Just what are you doing with Lambert?' Patrick asked. 'And why are you here?'

'I thought Dad would have written to tell you,' Megan said, after thanking Georgina and saying she would prefer a cold drink but no alcohol. 'It's a bit early,' Megan said, but Georgina laughed.

'I haven't heard from Dad for . . . for ages,' Patrick told her.

Megan wondered if he was lying. After all, that desperate, pleading letter had arrived only three weeks before and her father was sure to have written to reassure his beloved son!

'Dad's gone to live with Aunt Lily in Dorset,' Megan said.

72

'He must be mad!' exclaimed Patrick. Megan felt furious, for her father was sacrificing his freedom for Patrick. Surely Patrick must know that? 'But how does that bring you out here?' he added.

Megan sipped her ice-cold orange squash and looked round. The room was tastefully and expensively furnished. She liked the lilac shade of the walls, the deep red silk-covered armchairs, the polished floor with the beautiful rugs. It certainly didn't look like the home of a man so desperate for help that his father had to sell his own house! She stifled a sigh. Perhaps Patrick had been writing all these years for financial help when he didn't really need it and she and her father had sacrificed many things they enjoyed in order to help him.

'How did I get out here?' she said slowly. 'I've just told you that Dad has gone down to Dorset to live. That meant I had no home. I had to get a job, and . . .'

Georgina laughed. 'I bet you were glad to be free of the old man. A real hypochondriac, that's what he was.'

'He suffered a lot of pain,' Megan said quickly.

'Maybe, but he made use of it,' Georgina said. 'He adored being made a fuss of and you and Aunt Lily completely spoiled him. There was absolutely no need for you to stop your dancing just because he was lonely when you weren't there—and when you were, was he a real companion? His nose buried in the newspaper or his eyes glued to the telly,' Georgina went on, her voice sarcastic. 'You were so soft, you fell for it. He didn't *need* you—he just wanted to have someone around. Now he's got Aunt Lily.' She laughed. 'Aunt Lily is growing old—it won't be long before they send for you.'

Megan twisted her fingers together. So much of what Georgina said was true, but also so much untrue. Her father did like attention, but he needed help. He didn't need *her*—that she knew, now, and that was what hurt her so much. No one needed her. And to live a full life, you must be needed by someone.

'For crying out loud,' Patrick said impatiently, 'could we drop this cross-talk? Give Megan a chance to tell us what made her come out here.'

'Okay, okay, big brother.' Georgina curled up on the couch. 'Fire ahead, Megan. What are you doing here? Snooping on us?'

Megan coloured. She had been afraid they would think that—it seemed she was right!'

'Actually—and I know you won't believe me, but it's the truth—I got the job just by chance. I was teaching for Mrs Arbuthnot and she had had enquiries from the Lambert School who were looking for a teacher. This was quite a while ago.'

'Why . . . well, why should they go to a miserable little school like hers?' Patrick asked.

'It isn't a miserable little school,' Megan told him quickly. 'It's getting a very good name, because a lot of our pupils do well. Anyhow, the Lambert School did. Mrs Arbuthnot said nothing to me, because she knew I'd never walk out on Dad, but when I went to her and said I simply had to find a job, and I didn't see how I could for I'd had no proper training in teaching dancing, she notified the Lambert School.'

'What—wrote out here?' Georgina lit a cigarette slowly.

'No. They have a representative in London—Miss Wilmot.'

'And then?' Patrick was pacing the room, hands clasped behind his back, his head stuck forward, rather like a giraffe's, Megan thought, grateful for a moment of amusement, for she was not enjoying her afternoon. As she had feared, they didn't believe her.

'Then I was interviewed by Mr Lambert. Apparently he had watched me teaching—you remember Mrs Arbuthnot had that special kind of mirror.'

'To make sure the teachers were doing their stuff properly,' Georgina said nastily. She had taught in Mrs Arbuthnot's school for a short time, Megan remembered. A very short time, and that was where she met Patrick and married him.

'Well, it was while Mr Lambert was

75

interviewing me that I learned where the school was.'

'Mrs Arbuthnot hadn't told you?' Georgina asked, her voice disbelieving.

'No. I knew it was an exclusive school and that it was abroad. I'd hardly had time to think of asking where. Then when Mr Lambert told me, I realised it was here on the same island as you.'

'You told him?' Patrick snapped.

'Of course.' Puzzled, Megan looked from Georgina to Patrick and back to Georgina 'Naturally I told him. It seemed such a coincidence.'

'Coincidence my foot!' Patrick spluttered. 'It's all part of his plot to get rid of us. He's got you out here to use you against me, Megan. I'd have thought you'd have had more sense and decency to stay away.'

'I never thought of it. Why should I?' Megan asked. It was obvious that Patrick and Georgina were both being careful—they were wondering just how much her father had told her about Patrick's plea for help. After all, for all they knew, she might not have even seen the letter, much less have read it. In fact, unless they knew she had read the letter, they had no means of knowing that she had read what Patrick had said: that *Craig Lambert was determined to ruin him.*

She decided it was wiser to avoid involvement of any kind, so she looked at them

76

with an innocent smile.

'I don't understand. I'd no idea you would mind me coming out. After all, I am your sister and it was a very good job, and as far as I could see, there was no reason at all why I shouldn't take the job.'

Georgina leaned forward. 'She's right, Patrick. After all, she'd never heard of Craig Lambert, had you?'

'Of course not. Is he famous or something?' Megan looked her sister-in-law in the eyes. 'What is all this about, Georgina? Patrick's making me feel I've done something to hurt him in coming out here. After all,' she added bitterly, 'we needn't meet. I'm on the other side of the island.'

Patrick stormed out of the room, banging the door. Georgina shrugged. 'Poor Patrick! He's going through a difficult phase just now. Life here isn't being as rewarding as we had hoped, Megan. What made your father decide to sell the house so promptly?'

Sell the house, Megan thought instantly. So her father *had* written and, no doubt, sent them the money. She had not said anything about selling the house, only that her father had decided to live with Aunt Lily in Dorset! So they were both of them hiding the truth from her? Obviously they believed she knew nothing about Patrick's plea for help!

'I don't know,' she said, deciding to pretend she hadn't noticed Georgina's slip of the

77

tongue. 'He suddenly told me that Aunt Lily had asked him to go down to Dorset with her as she found it isolated and a man about the house could be a good defence.'

Georgina grunted. 'Fat lot of good he'd be as a defence! I know you're loyal, Megan, but honestly you were a fool to throw away your chance to become a good dancer. Mrs Arbuthnot had trained you well, and then . . .'

'Well, what else could I do when Aunt Lily walked out?'

'Couldn't your father have had a housekeeper?'

'A housekeeper!' Megan said scornfully. 'How could he afford it?'

She was so angry she made herself get up and go to the window, staring out blindly. When she thought of how Patrick had got money from her father—money they needed so badly themselves, and all the time he had been living in a house like this, with a maid and goodness knew what else . . .

'You like the house?' Georgina asked.

Megan forced herself to smile. 'Very nice. I like your view, too. It's a bit scruffy by the hotel.'

'Yes.' Georgina yawned. 'Bad management, there. I tore strips off Gaston for being such a fool as to leave it to the Piggots. Of course you don't know them. You never will unless you come and visit us,' she added. 'We live on the wrong side of the island, according to Craig

78

Lambert. What's he like?' Georgina asked suddenly, her voice changing, becoming almost wheedling. 'He's certainly not handsome.'

'No, but . . .' As usual, the need to defend whoever was attacked rose in Megan. 'Actually he can be kind, but he can also . . .'

'Be horrid? I'm surprised he engaged you. How did you tell him you were Patrick's sister?'

Megan returned to her chair and curled up in it. 'I told him as soon as he said the Lambert School was on an island near the Seychelles. I said at once that I had a brother out there somewhere, but I wasn't sure which island.'

'No.' Georgina pulled a wry face. 'I'm afraid we're not very good at writing letters, Megan.'

Only when you need money, Megan thought, and clenched her hands tightly.

'Was he angry, Megan?'

'Angry? Oh, you mean when I told him? No, I'd say he was startled.'

'You don't think he knew?' Georgina's voice had changed again; now it sounded cautious.

'I certainly don't because he didn't look at all pleased—nor was Miss Wilmot when I told her. I got the impression that Mr Lambert didn't like you being on the island.'

Georgina laughed. 'He lives in the past—or else he's crazy about money. He wants the whole island to himself. He can't open his eyes to see the possibilities here. It could become a great tourist centre. All he thinks of is himself.'

Here, Megan felt inclined to agree, but before she could say anything the door opened and Patrick walked in, followed by the most handsome man Megan had ever seen. He was the sort of man you saw on television and if you were that sort of person you swooned or shouted excitedly, for he was tall, lean, and dark, with long sideboards and thick hair and the most charming smile.

Now he came towards her, his hand held out in greeting.

'Ah, but this is wonderful! Patrick's young sister. I am delighted to meet you.' He shook her hand, his fingers curving tightly round hers as if desiring to pass on a message. His eyes shone. 'I am Gaston Duval. You have, it may be, heard of me, no?'

Megan caught her breath. Now she knew why Miss Wilmot had warned her to watch out! Anyone could fall for a man as attractive as this.

Not only was it his looks but his manners. He sat by her side, twisting round so that he could stare at her, letting his eyes seem to go slowly over all of her he could see, and then smiling at her with that secret look that told her that what he had seen, he had liked very much.

'Gaston came along,' Patrick was saying to Georgina, who was looking angry about something.

'But a coincidence,' Gaston said now, and

laughed. 'It is too strange, is it not? A coincidence,' he repeated. 'That you should be offered—ah, a very good position—in the island where your brother is.' He laughed. 'A strange coincidence, is it not so? Of all the islands, and there are many, in the world, fate chose this. There must be a reason.' He looked at the silent Patrick and Georgina. 'There can be nothing done but with a reason. We will find it.' He took Megan's hand in his, turning it to look at her palm. 'I tell fortunes. I am very good. Yes?' He looked at Georgina with a smile, but she didn't return the smile. 'Ah, Miss Crane—or may I call you Megan?' He said the name slowly, almost as if it was a caress. 'A beautiful name for a lovely girl,' he said, then looked at her hand. 'I see you have a character that is strong? That you are—how is it said— loyal to those you love, and even to those you do not love. Is it not?'

He smiled at her. Megan tried to concentrate on what he had said, and what it had meant. *Loyal to those you love and even to those you do not love.*

She wished as she had so often wished during the afternoon that Craig Lambert had left her alone, never brought her here to Patrick. She managed to remove her hand from Gaston's grasp without doing it too obviously and then looked at her watch.

'Mr Lambert is picking me up in ten minutes. Could I go and wash my hands,

81

Georgina? It's very humid.'

'Of course. This way.' Georgina led Megan down the corridor. Through half open doors, she saw two bedrooms, a very modern kitchen, and then she was in the bathroom. 'Do you like him?' Georgina asked as she showed Megan into the mirror-walled bathroom.

'Like him? Oh, you mean Mr Duval?' Megan turned on the water so that she could talk over her shoulder without letting Georgina see her face. 'He's very handsome, isn't he?'

'Yes, I suppose so. But I said did you *like* him?'

Megan turned. Now she could laugh. 'I've only known him for half an hour, Georgina. How can I know if I like him?' she asked.

Which wasn't true, of course. For she did know if she liked him! She liked him a great deal too much for her own comfort, that was the trouble.

*   *   *

Craig Lambert smiled as Megan joined him in the car. She didn't glance back, for she knew that neither Patrick, Georgina nor Gaston would be in sight. They had said goodbye to her and left her at the front door, closing it as soon as she moved outside.

'Enjoy yourself?' Craig Lambert asked, and there was an amused twinge in his voice she disliked.

She looked at him defiantly. 'Very much. I met Gaston Duval.'

If she had expected to surprise or anger Craig Lambert, she was disappointed, for he looked amused.

'I guessed he'd turn up. I trust you didn't fall for him as most females do. A bigger rogue I've yet to meet.' His voice was suddenly harsh.

'He has perfect manners,' Megan said quickly.

'Of course.' Craig Lambert's smile this time was cynical. 'That's part of his trade. His favourite line is to make some old lady think he adores her, then she leaves him all her money when she goes. He also has a devoted mother he drains. She, at least, has sense enough to avoid scandal, so keeps a firm hand on him.'

'That doesn't sound like him.' Megan turned to glare at her companion. 'Are you suggesting he kills the old ladies off?'

Craig Lambert laughed. 'Of course not. He's much too clever. He sees them as investments. He's a man who is completely amoral in every way. Your brother was a fool ever to have trusted him.'

'I . . .' Megan began, but stopped herself in time. She wasn't sure just how much she should say, so decided to say nothing.

There was a silence and then Craig Lambert spoke on his phone to the chauffeur, who nodded twice. No more was said for ten minutes and Megan was beginning to feel more and more uncomfortable. Craig Lambert's silences were always ominous. Was he annoyed because she had defended Gaston Duval? Would he tell her he found she was unsuitable for her position at the school?

She noticed they were going inland now, having left the coast road. That puzzled her, for that wasn't the way they had come. The road was winding and slowly rising, with trees on either side and large creepers of purple bougainvillea on every support, be it a house, fence or arch.

The car turned sharply to the right and Megan caught her breath. It couldn't be true . . . but it was. Her dream house was there . . . standing in front of them. A single-storied house with a thatched roof and a wide verandah, with flowers growing up the walls and a wide lawn stretching in front of it. Behind, the mountain grew larger, covered with trees, but here there were palm trees, upright as could be, and huge bushes of scarlet flowers.

'My house,' Craig Lambert said quietly.

'Yours?' She was really surprised. Somehow she had not imagined that Craig Lambert would choose such a simple house.

'Yes.' The car stopped. Megan prepared to get out, not quite sure why she was being taken to Craig Lambert's home. It was kind of him to

84

show her so much, but the next moment he was looking at her. 'I won't be a moment,' he said. 'I have to collect something.'

She sat back as if slapped. So he hadn't brought her here to show her his house. It was mere chance that she had seen it, for obviously the private life of Craig Lambert must never be mixed up with his public life. She looked round all the same. It was lovely—so quiet. The palm trees were just as she liked them, the flowers so lovely. How happy she could be here, she was thinking when Craig Lambert returned, spoke to the chauffeur and got in the car.

Craig Lambert ruffled through some papers he was holding, totally ignoring Megan until they got on the main road again.

'Well, what did you think of it?' he asked, looking at her.

'I thought it was lovely.'

He smiled. 'Aren't you being rather tactful? Most people think I'm mad to live there. I like it because it's so quiet. For once I can't hear the cackling of female laughter and their noisy chatter, nor the roar of the sea.'

'You live there?'

'Yes, I drive home every night and have a few hours of bliss. By the way,' he added, frowning a little, 'it might be as well not to mention to any of the staff that I took you there. They're already apt to see you as teacher's pet, which is why I avoid you at

85

school, for some of the staff are a funny lot—jealous, malicious, apt to alter the context of everything so that only the worst of it can be seen.' He spoke crisply, narrowing his eyes as he looked at her. 'I hear you're still good friends with Parr.'

'Of course I am. He's the nicest on the staff.'

'I thought he'd help you, that's why I was so nasty about him,' Craig Lambert said.

Megan twisted round on the seat. 'You . . . you said those things on purpose?'

Craig Lambert nodded. 'Of course. You're a strange female, Miss Crane, and have to be handled tactfully. I knew you'd need a friend, but I also knew if I recommended anyone, you'd run a mile to evade him. You're so convinced that I was ruthless, cruel, indifferent, and. your brother's enemy. Right?'

Megan didn't know what to do or say, for she knew her cheeks were betraying her as she looked at him in dismay.

Instead he smiled—his nice smile, this time. 'Don't look so upset, Miss Crane, I quite understand. Your brother is so dominated by Gaston Duval that he'll believe anything he's told. And I'm afraid you're the same.'

The car had reached the school and was slowing up. Megan got out slowly. What should she say? What was there to say? Craig Lambert knew everything.

As they went into the hall, Miss Tucker was

86

there talking to several of the staff. She looked a little surprised as she saw Megan come in with Craig Lambert by her side.

'I've been looking for you, Mr Lambert,' she said, a note of accusation in her voice.

'I had to go into town, so I gave Miss Crane a lift as she wanted to see her brother,' Craig Lambert explained.

Miss Tucker looked horrified. 'Her brother?' she repeated.

Megan looked at the tall ugly man by her side. 'Thank you for the lift,' she said politely, and escaped upstairs to the quietness of her room.

She went out on to the balcony, gazing at the beautiful blue sea, and drew a long deep breath. It had been quite an afternoon! She took out the folding chair she had found behind the bathroom door, unfolded it and sat in the late sunshine. Everything had that golden colour the world assumes as the sun goes slowly down. She buried her face in her hands, feeling absolutely muddled.

Now who was she to believe? Craig Lambert? Was he right when he said Gaston Duval was a rogue? Was it true that Gaston Duval was cheating and lying and had brain-washed Patrick into believing that Craig Lambert was his enemy?

Or was Patrick right in his belief that Craig Lambert was determined to get rid of everyone he disapproved of who lived on the island? Could Gaston Duval with his charming manner, his ability to make you feel beautiful and admired, to feel even breath-less after he had held her hand for a short time . . . could he be what might be called a 'baddie'? She found it hard to believe.

Or was it because she still could feel the warmth of his hand, the admiration in his eyes, the knowledge that here was a man, a real man.

Had she fallen in love with Gaston Duval? she asked herself. And if she had, then what would happen?

* * *

It seemed as if nothing was going to happen, for as the days passed, Megan's life became almost routine and she didn't meet Gaston. She began to relax and enjoy her new life. Craig Lambert avoided her; if they met he was coolly polite, but he didn't suggest giving her another lift to see her brother. Several of the staff had given Megan lifts into the small town, to shop or have coffee, but she never asked them to take her to the Crane Dancing Studio, for she had no desire to see either Patrick or Georgina. She was still so angry with both of them when she thought of the money they had got from her father and herself—money they obviously didn't need half as much as her father did.

The days passed swiftly. The weather was

perfect, for it was too early for the monsoon. Every day Megan found herself in one of the small coves that were below the school and where they all swam in the lagoon—a safe lagoon, as it had no opening to the Indian Ocean and the water came in with the high tides, tossing over the reef.

Of all the pupils she taught, Megan made few friends. She was not sorry about this, yet she found herself watching the girl Anarita Marco worriedly.

Anarita was always in trouble. It was true she asked for it, for she was defiantly rude and frequently refused to do what she was told.

'But Frank, she's seventeen,' Megan said one evening to him as they sat on in the big room where he taught them bridge.

'Seventeen or not, she isn't entitled to be damned rude,' he said crossly.

'She's unhappy here. She's much more mature than the other girls.'

'Then why does she stay here?' Frank gathered the cards together. 'There are other schools with less strict rules.'

'She has no choice,' Megan told him. 'Her parents are dead, she has a guardian who's about as out of date as the dodo. She can't do anything she wants until she's twenty-one and then she'll inherit . . .'

'A small fortune, which is why the guardian wants her to be protected,' Frank told her. 'He doesn't want any smart Tom, Dick or Harry to marry her and lay his hands on her wealth. Protection, Meg, not frustration—that's our motto.'

That was something Megan had learned since she came to teach dancing at the Lambert School. Many of the pupils were from European countries whose parents or grandparents had once been kings and queens. Others came from the East, of wealthy families who insisted on protection and proper behaviour. The strict rules of the school were part of the curriculum, not to harass the unfortunate girls but to protect them.

One day Megan had a chance to talk alone to Anarita.

'They don't mean to be unkind,' she explained.

'They just don't care. Nobody cares!' Anarita said angrily.

'I care,' said Megan.

Anarita gave her a strange look, her long black hair swinging. 'I believe you do,' she said, her voice surprised. 'Why?'

'Perhaps because I'm only three years older than you. Perhaps because I've known that same kind of frustration, wanting to do something I'm unable to do. I wasn't at school, I was looking after my father.' Megan told her about her life in Hastings, and Anarita, after that, often talked to her.

'If only we weren't shut up in here like a lot of young nuns!' Anarita said angrily. 'One day we've got to meet men, how long do we have to wait?' She sighed, twisting her long black hair round one hand slowly. 'After all, lots of girls marry when they are fifteen or sixteen. I ought to have a chance to meet men. I know what it is. My guardian, he seeks the right husband for me. He does not care in case I hate the man. Oh no, that is not important. Look, you read the magazines, you read the papers. Everywhere people love one another, but me . . . oh no, no question of love for me.'

'But he can't make you marry if you refuse, if you don't love the man,' Megan pointed out.

'I know, but then neither can I marry the man if he refuses permission—my guardian, I mean, of course. So . . . so I must wait until I am twenty-one. Four more years.' Anarita sighed. 'You are so lucky. In a year you will be twenty-one.'

In England now you can marry at eighteen, even if your parents disapprove.'

'Ah!' Anarita smiled. 'I wish my father had been English, then, for it would be only a year to wait.'

'You want to marry?'

'I want to marry, yes. I suppose I want to be *loved,*' Anarita said.

Megan found it hard to forget Anarita's pathetic words: *I want to be loved.*

It was purely by chance that Megan found herself alone with Craig Lambert one day. She had had a very energetic class, and when it was over, she had several hours before the next one, so she had gone outside into the sunshine, strolling down towards the golf course. Only the roar of the distant sea and the chatter of the birds broke the stillness. In many ways this was a realisation of her dream, her impossible dream, Megan was thinking, if only . . .

If only she had the answer to a few questions. Could she trust Craig Lambert—or should she believe Patrick and . . . and Gaston? Why had Mr Lambert dismissed Miss Pointer so suddenly? Had Mr Lambert deliberately, Megan wondered, brought her out here to use her as a weapon against her brother? If so, in what way could he use her?

She was asking herself this question, leaning against the sturdy trunk of a tree, watching two honey birds hovering like minute helicopters over the vividly yellow flowers. She was quite startled when a deep voice said:

'Dreaming—as usual?'

Craig Lambert! She turned round quickly. 'I didn't hear you.'

'You were miles away. What were you dreaming about?' he asked.

Megan hesitated. She couldn't tell him the truth—suddenly she knew this was the opportunity she thought she would never get.

'I was thinking about Anarita.'

'I've heard you seem to be getting on with her quite well. A pleasant change from hearing about her insolence and tantrums.'

92

'The girl is unhappy . . . she talks to me.'

'You are more or less the same age group, of course,' Craig Lambert said. 'I suppose she feels she can. What were you thinking about?'

She told him how Anarita felt, that she needed to be loved. 'She seems to have never had anyone to love her,' she said gravely.

'And now you've turned up?' Craig Lambert asked.

Megan was surprised. 'Well, I hadn't thought of it like that, but if she feels someone cares for her and wants her to be happy . . .'

'You think you can help her?'

'I can but try.'

'Okay. What do you want me to do?'

Megan hesitated. 'I don't honestly know. I was wondering if I could take her into town sometimes. We could go on the bus and . . .'

Craig Lambert's face changed; it might have been made of stone. Megan recognised the sign at once, for she had seen it so often.

'On one condition,' he began sternly.

Megan glared at him. 'You don't have to tell me, Mr Lambert. On one condition—*that you don't take her anywhere near your brother.* That's what you were going to say, wasn't it?'

Craig Lambert smiled, his face relaxing. 'Actually, for once you're quite wrong. I was going to say that you don't take her to the wrong side of the town. You know where I mean. This has nothing to do with your brother, but lately a rough crowd has turned

93

up there, whether for a holiday or to seek work, I don't know, but they're highly undesirable for our girls. Most of them are artists—but typical hippies. Our girls' parents would be horrified if they thought we allowed their daughters to mix with these creatures.'

'What's wrong with hippies?' Megan began, but Craig Lambert gave her no time.

'Two things; dirt and drugs. I'll run no risk of the girls being involved in such circumstances. I know what you're getting at and I agree that all hippies are not bad—but many are, and those many are the ones I will not let my girls mingle with. Understand?'

'Yes, you're right, of course,' Megan agreed. 'If you tell me where the border is, I promise you I won't let Anarita cross it.'

He told her, giving the name of a row of shops. 'Just stay in the main road and everything will be okay.'

'Should I . . . I mean, you did tell me I took my orders from Miss Tucker.'

Craig Lambert lifted his hand. 'Leave it to me. All the same, let Miss Tucker know. I'll see that it's all right,' he said, and strode off down the field.

Megan watched him go. He had taken that very well. It would be nice to take Anarita in, to encourage her to talk, to let her feel part of life.

So a new routine began. Whenever Megan was offered a lift into town, she asked if

Anarita could go with her, too. No one refused to take her, so then Megan would go to Miss Tucker for her permission.

'Personally I think you're wasting your time, Miss Crane,' Miss Tucker said the first time. 'That girl needs a good spanking. However, Mr Lambert thinks it's a good idea of his, so I must agree.'

Megan had hurried away, trying to hide her smile. Mr Lambert! Cunningly pretending it was *his* idea, for he knew very well how Miss Tucker resented accepting any of the staff's suggestions.

These trips into town were great fun, Megan found. So did Anarita, who loved going round the shops with Megan while they discussed and argued about what clothes they thought were 'with it'. Or to stand in the market and watch the Creole women selling their goods, the tiny dark-coloured babies smiling away, showing their tiny white teeth, and the small children playing in the dust.

'Thanks to you I feel part of the world,' Anarita said one day.

'But you've been into town before?' Megan asked.

'Oh yes, but with some dull old cow.'

'Anarita!' Megan had to laugh even while she scolded. 'That's not a nice word.'

Anarita looked very innocent. 'Isn't it? But the Aussies use it.'

'Yes, but not as a compliment. And we're

95

not Aussies.'

They had their favourite café and would sit under the bright sunshades on the pavement outside, watching the people go by.

'You're not an old cow,' Anarita said once. 'Not even a young cow.'

Megan had to laugh. 'Thanks. What am I, then?'

'Nice,' was all Anarita said, but it was enough to make Megan's cheeks glow with pleasure.

Occasionally in the crowd Megan would lose sight of Anarita, but always saw her later, standing outside a shop waiting for her.

'Where did you get to?' Anarita would ask, her eyes amused as she saw Megan's anxious face.

'Looking for you,' Megan said.

Anarita laughed. 'You don't need to worry, Megan. I can look after myself.'

'Mr Lambert doesn't think so.'

'Mr Lambert!' Anarita said scornfully. 'Pity he's so square, for he's terribly attractive.'

'Attractive?' Megan was surprised. 'I think he's very ugly.' Her hand flew to her mouth. 'Oh dear, I shouldn't have said that!'

Anarita's eyes twinkled. 'You shouldn't, because I shall tell my friends and the whole school will know Miss Crane thinks Mr Lambert is very ugly.'

'Anarita, please,' Megan begged. 'Please!'

'All right,' Anarita promised reluctantly, 'but

it's a shame, because they're all talking about you. We thought you and Mr Lambert were in love. I mean, it was odd you coming so soon after Miss Pointer left, wasn't it?'

'Pure chance,' Megan said quickly. 'I keep meaning to ask you, Anarita, why do you speak such perfect English when you are Italian?'

'But I'm really English, it's just that my father was Italian. He was never at home and I lived with my mother in Venice, but we always talked English at home. Then they both died and . . . they sent me here.'

'How long have you been here?'

Anarita sighed. 'Too long. Far too long. Ever since I was ten.'

'It is a long time,' Megan agreed.

Often, she found herself thinking about her brother Patrick. After all, even if they didn't get on well, they were brother and sister. Yet obviously he had no desire to see her even though she was so near.

Actually she had been thinking this one day as she swam in the warm sea with Frank. Or rather, Frank sat on the beach and watched her. He was, he had said, allergic to salt water. Although he had laughed, Megan wondered if it was the real reason.

Now as she floated on her back happily, she thought how wonderful it would be if Patrick and Craig Lambert could become friends; if the strange mystery she had somehow become involved in as to why she was out here could be

97

solved.

This job was indeed her 'impossible dream' for the staff seemed to have accepted her, and the classes were proving most satisfactory and she was amazingly happy—but there was always this business of Patrick and Craig Lambert. Not to forget, her conscience reminded her, Gaston Duval. She could not forget him, somehow. She just could not.

Walking up to the school, talking to Frank, Megan wished she could trust him and tell him everything. Was it all her imagination? Was it simply a question of Craig Lambert being naturally annoyed at losing part of the island he so obviously treasured?

When she got back to the school, Frank walked on as she hovered round the board where the letters were stuck. She had not heard once from her father or Aunt Lily. Megan had written several times and although she knew her family were bad letter writers she couldn't help feeling worried and a little hurt, but there was a letter for her this time. But it wasn't from England. It was posted in Coeur Mêlé, the small town nearby.

Puzzled, she opened it. It was a printed invitation, inviting her to a champagne party at the Crane Dancing Studio on the seventeenth. In writing was added; 'Bring your boy-friend, too, if you like. Patrick '.

What was she to do? she wondered. Was she, as well as the pupils, barred from the wrong side of the town? Did she want to go? Gaston would surely be there.

She looked up and saw Craig Lambert walking by. She ran after him, 'Mr Lambert!' she called a little breathlessly.

He turned to stare at her. 'What's the trouble this time?' he asked.

'I don't know what to do. My brother has invited me to a party and to take a friend. Would you mind . . . ?'

'If you went?' he asked. 'Of course not. You're an adult, presumably capable of protecting yourself. I only meant the pupils when I said it was banned. On the seventeenth, is it? I hope you'll enjoy it,' he said. 'Time you met a few more people,' he added as he walked away.

Megan stood still for a moment, gazing at the card in her hand. Who could she take with her? What had Patrick meant when he said *your boy-friend?*

CHAPTER IV

The invitation continued to puzzle Megan, for surely Patrick could have written a letter or phoned her? What had Patrick meant, too, when he wrote 'boy-friend'? The only real friend she had at Lambert School—masculine, that was, and at a party you usually took a man—was Frank. She wondered how he would

99

react.

She chose a good moment. She had come out of the warm sea and the drops were trickling down her as she dried herself. Frank, his straw hat tilted over his eyes as he lay on his back on the sand, said:

'What's worrying you, Meg?'

She sat down by his side, looking along the Cove. Groups of the girls were swimming or sunbathing with Miss Weston in charge. Miss Weston, though she had the flat next to Megan's, had had little to do with her. Always polite, yet there was a coldness in her smile. Even now, she was sitting with her back to them when she could easily enough have come to sit with them.

'I've been invited to a party at my brother's dancing school,' Megan explained.

Frank was so startled he sat up. 'Good grief! Lambert won't be very pleased about that.'

Megan had begun to dry her hair which was hanging down over her face, so she parted it to look at him.

'He didn't seem to mind.'

'You asked him?'

'Of course.' Megan tossed her hair back and smiled. 'I had no choice, had I?'

'And he didn't blow his top?'

Megan laughed. 'Of course he didn't. He said he hoped I'd enjoy myself, that it was a good idea for me to meet more people . . . and that, though that part of the island was banned to the girls here, he thought I was mature enough to protect myself.'

'Golly!' Frank pretended to groan. 'Just how pompous can he get? He's wrong, though, you know. You're not at all mature, you're a foolish little romantic. I wouldn't let you loose at that party with all the gigolos and whatnots.'

'What do you mean, *whatnots?*' Megan pulled up her legs, rested her chin on her knees and turned her head to look at him.

She could see Miss Weston staring down their way and quickly looking away again as she scolded one of the girls. They were gathered round her as if prepared to go back to the school, for it was nearly tea-time.

What do I mean by whatnots?' Frank repeated the words slowly as if making time in which to think. 'I don't mean anything nasty, just that the Crane School supplies the hotel with male and female dance hosts so that all the tourists, no matter what their age, can be sure of a pleasant evening. Actually I was thinking of the biggest gigolo of them all: Gaston Duval.'

'Gaston?' Megan stretched out her legs and turned angrily. 'He's not a gigolo!'

'So you've met him?' Frank ran his hand through his hair. 'Ye gods and little fishes—does Mr Lambert know that?'

'Yes. I told him so,' Megan said defiantly.

'And he still lets you go to that party?' Frank shook his head. 'Either he's crackers or he

101

wants to get you into trouble.'

'Frank, that's not a nice thing to say,' Megan began angrily, then paused. The main thing she wanted to ask him had still not been said. 'Frank, I can take a boy-friend. I wondered if you'd come with me.'

'Me?' Frank gasped. 'Me? Well, I . . .'

'I know you're not my boy-friend, Frank,' Megan said quickly. 'But you are my best friend and I always feel so safe when I'm with you.'

He gave her a hard, long look. 'Thanks for the compliment,' he said drily.

'Well, to be honest, Frank, I need your help.' Megan curled up on the sand so that she was facing him and no longer staring at the calm blue lagoon. 'My brother and I—my sister-in-law, too—don't really talk the same language. I'm going to feel awfully alone there.'

'With Gaston Duval?' Frank asked sarcastically. 'I doubt if he'd give you time to breathe.'

'Oh, Frank, do please listen. There's also the problem of transport.'

'Ah, now I really understand! You want me to be your chauffeur?' Frank began to laugh. 'I'm only teasing, Meg. The real thing that stops me going is that I can't dance.' He waggled his right foot. 'I was in a car crash once and my foot was badly crushed. It's not a pretty sight.'

'Is that why you don't swim?'

'Yes, I'm too proud, I'm afraid. I also hurt my hip—that's why I walk so badly. You must have noticed.'

'I didn't. I noticed you limped a little, but ..' Megan laughed. 'Look, Frank, this is a party and not a dancing competition. If you take me, you haven't got to dance. Just . . .'

'Keep an eye on you, eh? Drive you there and back and watch a mass of handsome young males fighting for your company.'

'Frank . . .' Megan paused. 'Look, I'm not all that keen to go so if you'd rather not, say so.'

'Then you won't go?' Frank scrambled to his feet, leaning heavily on his right hand as he did so, and beginning to collect the towels.

'Not without you,' Megan got up, too, putting on her short towelling coat.

'You win,' Frank said as they turned to walk up towards the school.

'Bless you!' smiled Megan. 'Think you should tell Mr Lambert?'

Frank went bright red. 'I do not think anything of the sort. There are limits to what I'll accept.'

'Why are you here, Frank?' she asked as they got nearer the school. 'Mr Lambert told me you were a very fine artist.'

'Sweet of him, I'm sure,' Frank joked, then frowned. 'I wanted to be an artist, but there comes a moment in one's life when you realise it's just a dream . . .'

'An impossible dream?' Megan asked eagerly.

Frank nodded. 'Yes. I discovered I could never be *a real* artist. The next best thing was to help youngsters have the training I had and that I failed to use.'

'But why did you choose girls? I'd have thought . . .'

'Because I like girls, you idiot,' Frank was saying as they went through the swing door into the corridor.

Several of the girls ahead turned to stare at them and then put their heads together, their laughter sounding as they ran away.

'Boys are so exhausting,' Frank said, mimicking a sing-song voice.

'And girls are such chatterboxes,' said Megan, knowing that within an hour it would be all over school that Mr Parr had called Miss Crane an idiot! Anyhow, her problem was solved. 'Thanks, Frank,' she said as she turned to go up the back staircase. It really led to the girls' part but it was a short cut to her flat.

'My pleasure,' he said, looking up from below and smiling.

For a moment, she felt worried. Frank couldn't possibly be falling in love with her, could he? she asked herself. They were such good friends . . . she needed him so badly for in the difficulties of this school life; he made all the difference in the world for her.

She showered and dressed quickly, then wrote an acceptance for the party invitation. 'I'm bringing a friend with me,' she wrote.

When Megan ran down to the dining-room she was stopped in the hall by Craig Lambert. How ugly he was, she thought, as he beckoned to her. How different from Frank who, for all his insignificant look, at least had a pleasant face.

'Are you going to the party?' Craig asked curtly. Megan showed him the letter in her hand that she was going to drop into the hall box. 'Yes.'

'You've got a boy-friend?'

'I've got *a friend,*' she said.

A smile seemed to crack the sternness of Craig Lambert's face. 'I'm glad,' he said, turning away. 'Now I needn't worry.'

She watched him walk down the hall and then she went to the letter box, frowning a little. Why had he said that? Had he been worried? If so, why had he consented to her going in the first place? she wondered.

Much to Megan's surprise, next day Miss Weston said she was driving into town that afternoon, and would Megan like to go. They were talking just outside the building, watching the girls play tennis before lunch.

'Thanks, I'd love to go,' Megan said eagerly. It always made a change. Much as she liked her pupils, there was always a noise at the school, apart from the tension caused by the unfriendliness and obvious criticism of the members of the staff who had still not completely accepted her. 'Can I bring Anarita?'

'Of course. She's your shadow, isn't she? Do you think it's a good idea to let her become so dependent on you?' Miss Weston asked.

'It was Mr Lambert's idea,' Megan said meekly—which wasn't quite the truth, but as that was what he had told Miss Tucker it must be backed.

Miss Weston looked annoyed. 'I can't understand why he chose a newcomer like you when most of us knew her so well and for so long.'

Megan gave a quick look at Miss Weston's face. 'I think it was because of the age group,' she said, and then realised she had made a terrible mistake, for Miss Weston looked furious.

'I'm not completely senile yet, Miss Crane,' Miss Weston snapped. 'I'm only just thirty.'

'But you're Mr Lambert's age group, aren't you?' Megan said seriously, trying to repair the damage she had done. 'I mean, I'm just twenty, and that is much nearer seventeen, isn't it?'

'I suppose so . . .' Miss Weston said reluctantly. 'But I would have thought she'd feel more at ease with us when she's known us for so long.'

'Perhaps too long?' Megan suggested. 'I'm someone new—and someone new usually gets the interest to start with. I expect she'll soon get tired of me, too.'

'Indeed? Well, don't keep me waiting, at three o'clock, sharp,' Miss Weston said. 'I have to go to the dentist. Frightful nuisance.'

'Poor you,' Megan said sympathetically. 'Well, I'll go and see Anarita.'

She had quite a search for the girl and finally found her in the library, talking to several other girls. There was a sudden silence as Megan came through the wide swinging glass doors, so she knew they had been talking about her!

'Anarita,' Megan said as she walked up to them, 'I'm going to town this afternoon. Like to come?'

'Who's driving us?' Anarita, her long black hair swinging back, asked.

'Miss Weston.'

'Whew, that's a change, isn't it?' Anarita laughed. 'I think this is the first time my Lady Weston has condescended to take me in. What's happened?'

'Anarita, there's no need to be rude,' Megan said quickly. 'It's very good of Miss Weston. If you'd rather not come, then just say so.'

'Of course I want to come—with you,' said Anarita.

'Good—then two-forty-five this afternoon. Right?'

'Right,' Anarita said with a smile.

Megan walked to the dining-room. She was

107

the first to sit down at the staff table. The quietness vanished as the girls came tumbling in, all talking at the top of their voices. Gradually the staff table filled up, Frank by her side.

'You're looking very thoughtful,' he teased. 'What's wrong this time?'

'Nothing,' Megan told him. 'Just something that puzzles me.'

'Be my guest—I'm good at solving problems.'

'I don't think you could solve this one,' she said.

Later as she changed into a clean dress in her flat, Megan thought again how odd it was that Miss Weston had suddenly offered her a lift. Why—when for all these past weeks, Miss Weston had barely spoken to her, and certainly not at all unless she was so obliged. Why now?

Could Mr Lambert have asked her to check up on Megan's behaviour? To watch what happened when Megan and Anarita went to town? Megan had an uncomfortable feeling that she was constantly under supervision, but perhaps it was absurd. After all, why should Craig Lambert want a report of all she did?

Unless he still distrusted her and believed she was working for her brother?

Working for him? Just how stupid can you be? she asked herself. In what way could she *work* for him?

As she hurried downstairs, glancing anxiously at her watch, for she had deliberately told Anarita an earlier time because the Italian-English girl seemed to delight in keeping people waiting; Megan herself wanted to be there first, as it was in some small way setting an example.

She had just reached the curve in the wide staircase when she saw Craig Lambert coming up the stairs, two at a time. As he saw her, he stopped.

'Ah, just the person I wanted to see,' he said curtly. 'I've had a letter from your Mrs Arbuthnot. How come you've never written to her?'

Megan's hand flew to her mouth. 'I meant to, but I forgot. I'm . . . I'm not a very good letter writer.'

'That's no excuse at all. She's anxious about you, eager to know how you've adapted yourself. How have you?'

'I'm very happy here,' Megan told him.

'You get on all right with everyone? The children, pianists, staff?'

Megan moistened her lips. 'In a way, very well.'

He smiled, his face relaxing. 'I get the message. And in a way, not. By the way, Mrs Arbuthnot said an old friend had phoned up asking for your address. A . . . a Leontine Harrap.'

'Leo?' Megan exclaimed. 'I haven't heard from her for ages. Her parents went to Australia.'

'That must have been when you were at Everglades, I suppose.'

'Yes, it was.' Megan paused, staring at him, puzzled. 'But how do you know that? I never told Mrs Arbuthnot about it, as she and Mrs Harding who ran Everglades Dancing School were rivals. I was only there one term and I hated it—that's why I left and went to Mrs Arbuthnot, but how could she know?'

A smile crossed his face—a smile that annoyed her, for it was not only amused but sarcastic. 'Mrs Arbuthnot didn't have to tell me. I know all about you, Miss Crane, right back to the day and place you were born. Excuse me.' He walked by her and then turned. 'Would you please write to Mrs Arbuthnot and give her my best wishes, but I'm rather busy. I've got to go over to the Mainland tomorrow for a few days.'

And then he was gone, almost flying up the stairs. Megan stayed where she was for a moment, her hand clutching the banister. He knew everything about her, he had said? Everything—right back to the time and place she was born?

But why? He had no right . . .

She went down the stairs slowly. In other words, he had collected what she believed was called a *dossier.* But this was no cloak-and-dagger business, no F.B.I. or whatever it was in detective stories. Why—why had he to know everything about her?

She was still trembling with anger as she went outside. Anarita was there first, a triumphant smile on her lovely face.

'Beat you to it, Miss Meg!' she said happily.

'Yes, you did.'

'Something wrong?' Anarita asked.

Megan managed a smile. 'No—not really.' She looked round her at the colourful garden and the distant blue water. 'It's very beautiful here, isn't it, Anarita?'

'I suppose so,' Anarita shrugged. 'I'm getting awfully tired of it. I often have to spend my holidays here, too, you know.'

'You don't?' Megan was shocked.

Anarita laughed. 'It's not as bad as it sounds. Miss Tucker goes off and Mr Lambert takes over. He takes us for super schooner trips to the other islands, and twice we went by air to Mombasa, which was great fun.'

Mr Lambert does that? Himself?'

Anarita laughed. 'Yes. He doesn't half yell at us if we don't obey, but the rest of the time he's really rather sweet. He's a lonely man, you know.'

'Lonely?' Megan echoed. 'How do you mean, lonely?'

Turning to stare at Megan, Anarita laughed. 'You know what I mean all right. Any woman is lonely without a man—and any man lonely without a woman. The staff all chase poor Mr Lambert, and I don't blame him for keeping them at a distance. Apart from you, they're a lot of real duddies.'

'Indeed, how interesting!' Miss Weston's voice was sharp as she joined them. 'The car is round the back.'

It was a quiet journey into the small town. Megan tried to think of something to say, yet she and Miss Weston had nothing in common. Anarita on the back seat neither spoke or moved. She seemed to be ignoring them both.

Miss Weston left them at the market.

'I'll pick you up here in an hour's time,' she said as Megan and Anarita got out.

'Thank you,' Megan said with a smile. 'We'll be here.' She turned to Anarita as the car moved away. 'Now look, you're not to *lose* me today!'

'I don't lose you, you lose me,' Anarita laughed.

They wandered round the market with the huge bowls of fruit and great bunches of sweet-smelling flowers, the crowds of people either hurrying along or milling round the goods for sale. Twice Megan lost Anarita and she was getting a bit annoyed the last time she found her looking in an antique shop window.

'Anarita,' she said firmly, 'you must not leave my side. I'm responsible for you.'

'Oh, Miss Meg, do grow up,' Anarita said with her sweetest smile. 'Look I'm seventeen, going on for eighteen and this is the 1970s, not the Victorian age. What harm could be done to me?'

Megan hesitated. She didn't want to suggest that what Mr Lambert had said was right; any of these wealthy girls could be good for kidnapping. 'Please, Anarita, it is my responsibility.'

The girl smiled. 'I'll try, but you're so slow . . . you're too gentle in a crowd. You should just push your way through them, using your elbows,' she said. Then she clapped her hands. 'I'm dying for a cold drink. Let's sit at the café by the church. It looks rather nice.'

Megan hesitated for a moment. The church was very close to what Mr Lambert had described as the *banned area*—but still, it was on the *right* side!

'Okay,' she said. Anything was better than losing sight of Anarita!

They had a good view of the market at the end of the road, and the cars and bicycles going by as well as the strange little carts drawn by the Creoles. There always seemed so many people in the town, and as they sat under the bright-coloured sunshade at the small table, Megan and Anarita talked again about her childhood. It was certainly a sad one, Megan thought. She had always been sorry for herself, but now she felt sorrier for Anarita.

Megan was glancing at her watch, for Miss Weston must not be kept waiting—or *that* would be reported to Mr Lambert, no doubt, Megan thought bitterly—and soon they ought to go.

'May I join you?' a deep masculine voice said.

Megan turned and saw herself staring at a hippie, as undoubtedly Mr Lambert would have called him. The long, brown hair that came down his back was beautifully silky and he was wearing a thin crimson silk jacket and purple trousers.

'There isn't another table,' he said pathetically.

It was true. All the tables had filled. 'We're going in a moment,' Megan said, 'so do sit down.'

'I'm Tracy Thompson,' he said, holding out his hand and shaking Megan's, then turning to Anarita.

'Hullo,' she said coldly, hardly letting her hand touch his and turning away.

Megan sighed. Why had Anarita always to be so rude? To try to make up for it, she chatted to the hippie. Even if he was one, he was a very nice one, and anyway, what was wrong with being a hippie? she thought. Everyone has a right to have a personality of his or her own . . .

'I'm an artist,' he told them. 'Marvellous views here. You on holiday?'

'I work here,' Megan said, 'and . . . and . . .'

Anarita turned her head and looked at him contemptuously.

'I'm a schoolgirl,' she said, her voice bitter.

Tracy Thompson's eyebrows were lifted in

114

surprise. 'What, at the famous Lambert School? How do you like it?'

'Not much,' Anarita said, and turned away. 'We'd better go, Miss Meg. I'll pay this time,' she said as she stood up and walked into the café.

Megan hesitated and stared after the girl. 'I teach dancing at the school and . . .'

What's your name?' He smiled at her.

'Megan.'

'Welsh?'

No, but my grandmother was.'

They both laughed. Anarita returned, looking impatient.

Megan said goodbye and hurried after Anarita. They got to the market much too early. They talked as they waited and finally Megan said:

'I thought he was rather nice.'

'I thought he was pretty ghastly. So immature. I prefer older men,' said Anarita.

Maybe it was as well, Megan was thinking, as Miss Weston's car came into view, for Mr Lambert would certainly not approve of a friendship between Anarita and Tracy Thompson!

Back at the school, Megan was alone in her flat when there came a knock on the door. She had just showered and was in her thin, psychedelic-coloured housecoat, her hair hanging wetly round her face.

It was Craig Lambert. His eyes narrowed,

his voice low, tense with anger as he strode into the room, slamming the door behind him and swinging round to stare at her.

'I thought I could trust you!'

Megan stared back. 'You can.'

'A fine example of it, then. Why were you and Anarita sitting with that ghastly-looking hippie?'

'We were not sitting with him. There were no seats and he asked if he could join us. As we were just leaving, I said of course. I could hardly have refused, could I?' Megan asked.

'He bought you cold drinks?'

'Of course he didn't. He . . . or rather we weren't there long enough.'

'He asked for your names?'

'No. He told us his . . . oh, and he asked me mine. Anarita went to pay the bill and . . .'

'Of course you told him yours,' Craig Lambert said sarcastically.

'I only said Megan. I didn't give him Anarita's name at all. In any case, how do you know? Did you send Miss Weston to snoop on me?' Megan's anger was mounting fast. 'I hate all this spying. Why do you do it? Either you trust me or you don't. If you don't, I'll go!' she almost shouted the words at him.

Craig Lambert turned away, his hand on the door handle.

'I doubt if your brother would want you to do that,' he said drily. 'Why not ask him when you see him,' he added, and left the room.

Megan stood still, hugging herself angrily. He had no right . . . no right at all. She was tired of all this stupid . . .

He had no right at all. She hated him. She had a sudden impulse to get out her suitcases and pack all her things and go home . . .

Home?

She took a deep breath. That was something she hadn't got.

*   *   *

When the day of the party came, Megan was rather worried whether she was doing the right thing or not by going. But Craig Lambert had agreed, had even thought it a good idea. She and Frank decided it was best to keep it to themselves, so no one was told, and as Megan left her flat Petronella Weston, going into hers, lifted her eyebrows.

'Going to a party?' she asked, sounding surprised. 'I didn't . . .'

Megan smiled. 'Yes,' she said, and hurried down the corridor, giving Miss Weston no time to ask with whom! She was quite capable of doing so, and Frank had suggested that if asked, Megan could say simply that she was going out with him.

'That'll give the girls something to talk about,' Megan said, and laughed.

'Do you mind?' Frank asked, suddenly serious.

117

'Not really. It's not malicious chatter.'

'That's true,' he had agreed.

Now as she ran down the beautiful curved staircase, Megan thought how different it seemed without Craig Lambert there. He had gone to the Mainland, she knew, but for how long? Everything changed when he was away, she had noticed. Somehow or other he kept the peace, kept everything even, but since he had gone there were small quarrels among the staff, and a considerable number of arguments with Miss Tucker.

Frank was waiting in his car outside. He leaned over and opened the door for her.

'So you made it,' he grinned. 'Did the old dragon see you?'

'No, but Miss Weston did.' Megan snuggled down into the seat. 'She obviously longed to ask me who I was going with, but I just ran.'

He laughed as he started the car. 'Probably tomorrow Miss Tucker will send for you and say: "We do not allow affairs amongst the staff . . ."' He mimicked her voice well.

'So what? I shall tell her we're not having an affair, we're just good friends. Look, surely a man and a woman can be good friends without getting involved?'

Frank took a difficult corner carefully, for the night was pitch dark with not even a slice of moon to light the sky.

'A man and woman, yes, I agree—but a girl and a man? I wonder,' he said.

'Oh, let's forget them all, Frank,' said Megan, sliding down the seat so that she could lean against him. 'Let's just enjoy ourselves. I'm a bit worried about going and . . .'

'Because of me?'

'Goodness, no. You're my . . . what shall I call you? My guardian. It's just that . . . well, Mr Lambert and Patrick don't get on and . . .'

'Mr Lambert said you should go.'

'I know. That's what worries me.' Megan hesitated. As often before, she wished she could tell Frank everything, hear him sort it out in his humorous practical way and help her to see sense. Yet something always stopped her. 'I expect it'll be all right,' she added quickly, lying back in the seat and half closing her eyes.

She imagined she was looking at Craig Lambert's house. She wished she could tell Frank about that—wished she could describe the beauty and peacefulness of the thatched house, with the palm trees standing so gracefully and with no sign of violence in their straight trunks. She had fallen in love with the house as soon as she saw it. It had been almost uncanny, for it was just what she had always seen in her impossible dream. A strange house, she had thought, and still did, for a man like Craig Lambert. A romantic house, in a way, and he had said how he loved the quiet stillness of it. Yet he was such a virile man, a man knowing just where he was going and making for it, regardless of obstacles that he swept out of his way.

'Are both Mr Lambert's parents dead, Frank?' she asked.

'Yes. It was a good thing his father died when he did or there'd be no school today. Poor Craig. He was in South America, making a fortune on his own—I'm not sure how, but everything that man touches turns to gold. Then his father died and his mother sent for him. She was desperate, because she had just discovered about her husband's gambling and wasn't sure quite how much of the island *was* left to them. This was about eight years ago when he was in his early twenties. He really worked hard at it. You've got to hand it to him, Meg. He's a hard worker and expects the same of others and somehow gets it out of them. All seemed to be going well, then his mother was ill and passed on. We all wondered what Craig would do—sell the lot? Because he wasn't the type of man really to run a school. At least, you wouldn't think he was, yet he's surprisingly successful. He generates confidence, makes the anxious parents feel they can trust him—and trust him, they can,' Frank said.

'So he didn't sell the school?'

'No. He began bringing it up to date. His main pain in the neck is Miss Tucker, of course. I wonder he doesn't get rid of her. Mind, she's been with the school for some fifteen years. She was a close friend of his parents and bitterly resents any suggestion that the success of the school is due to Craig. She likes to think it is herself that has done it. Ah, this is where we get close to danger,' Frank chuckled as they reached the town. 'Might do Miss Tucker a bit of good to go to Paris, or better still, Hamburg, if she wants to see a bit of *real* night life. Ever been?'

'No. This is the first time I've been out of England.'

Megan was busy looking at the lighted shops and the groups of people chatting and laughing. The locals were a happy lot, she thought, so often singing and nearly always joking.

Now they were driving past the hotel that was ablaze with light, throwing shadows on the brightly-lighted Front and then they reached the Crane Studio. Frank parked his car and took Megan's arm. It was so hot that she had merely put a thin shawl over her shoulders. She was wearing a white dress, sleeveless and backless. She had been surprised when Miss Wilmot had chosen it.

'You'll be so hot out there,' Miss Wilmot had said, and how right she was!

The Studio was a very big hall that could be divided into different rooms with folded-back louvre doors. It seemed to be packed with people, standing and sitting, some dancing, others drinking.

Frank and Megan hesitated as they went in

121

and then Georgina came towards them. She looked even lovelier than usual in a deep red dress.

'Megan, how nice to see you!' she smiled, holding out her hands, surprising Megan, who wasn't used to such friendliness from her sister-in-law. 'And this is . . .?' She looked at Frank, puzzled.

'Frank Parr, an artist,' Megan said. 'Frank, this is my sister-in-law, Mrs Crane.'

'You must come and have something to eat,' Georgina told them, and led the way towards the long tables covered with plates of food, round which the guests were standing. 'I thought you were bringing Craig Lambert,' she whispered to Megan.

'Craig Lambert? Why should I? You didn't invite him.'

'We said your boy-friend. He is, isn't he? He seems to let you do a lot he won't let the others. For instance, always bringing that Anarita Marco into town.'

'You know her?' Megan was startled.

'Everyone's heard of her. She used to come in, of course, but not so often as she does now. How do you and Craig Lambert get on?'

'He employs me,' Megan said coldly.

Georgina laughed. 'You haven't changed—just as prickly! Come, Frank, because I can't call you Mr Parr, come and get us some drinks.'

Later Megan was standing alone when, to

her surprise, Patrick came up.

'Come and dance. It's many a year since we took to the floor together,' he said quite cheerfully, taking her by the hand and leading her to the dance floor.

His arm went round her and they were off . . . from then on, it was a nightmare for Megan. She knew Patrick was doing everything in his power to make her dance badly, or bungle it and look a fool.

He tried everything. Every trick that luckily she knew so well and how to combat and even anticipate. If only she was in Craig's arms, she found herself thinking.

That startled her, for it was the first time she had thought of him as *Craig* and not *Craig Lambert*. Now what had made her do that? Was it the memory of the wonder of the dance she had shared with him? the strength of his arm, the courtesy of his leading, the . . . togetherness, there was no better word for it, the togetherness of dancing. She couldn't forget it. She would never forget it.

This was the exact opposite. It was a battle—one she was determined to win.

As the music stopped, Patrick let her go. He looked thoughtful.

'You're a darned good dancer, Meg,' he said, sounding surprised. 'You're wasting your time teaching kids. You could make a fortune if you became a professional.'

'I'm happy where I am.'

They walked back towards the buffet tables. 'I can't get it. How can you stand that man?' said Patrick, his voice disgusted. 'It must be a nightmare to have him always prowling around.'

'He doesn't prowl around!'

'That's what you think, Meg. I bet he knows every single thing about you.'

Megan felt herself blush. Patrick was so right. 'He may have a reason,' she said stiffly. 'At this sort of school, you've got to be careful who you employ.'

'Too right,' Patrick laughed. 'So you're one of the chosen few. All the same, I wouldn't work for him. Rather starve. You just can't trust the man.'

'Patrick, Dad told me you said Mr Lambert had . . . well, nearly ruined you. What did he do?'

She saw the shock on her brother's face. 'Dad shouldn't have told you.'

'He was worried about you and very upset. But I want to know what Mr Lambert did.'

Patrick lifted his hand and waved to someone. 'It's too long a story to tell you now, Meg. Next time you come over, I will. Now Georgina and I have to dance. We give exhibition dancing always at the hotel on Saturday nights, you know, so this is an extra. Georgina and I are very popular. See you!'

Gradually the room was cleared, the guests standing or sitting in a big circle, leaving the centre of the room for the two dancers.

Megan leant against a wall and watched. Patrick was still as good a dancer, but this time he was dancing differently from the way he had danced with her! She could see how he guided Georgina. He was undoubtedly the strongest. But Georgina was graceful and good and they deserved the wild applause they got as they finished the different dances and then bowed to the audience.

'Megan—*ma chérie,* for you I have been looking,' a deep voice said, and she turned to find Gaston Duval by her side.

Something inside her seemed to be doing a wild dance. She decided it was her heart. It wasn't fair that any man should be so handsome.

'Hullo,' she said, trying to keep her voice calm.

His hand closed over her arm, sliding down it to take her hand in his and lift it to his mouth.

'I saw you dance with Patrick. Very good, you were. You are wasting your life at that school, my little Megan. You are too good a dancer.'

Megan laughed. 'That's what Patrick said, but I like my job.'

'This is something I have no power to understand,' Gaston said, leaning against her a little, his hand still holding hers tightly. 'How can you work—with that pig?' he added angrily.

'Look, Mr Lambert isn't . . .'

125

'Excuse me, Megan, it's time we went back,' a voice said.

Gaston seemed to jump, dropping Megan's hand as if it burned him. 'And who is this?' he asked.

'Frank Parr, my . . . my friend,' said Megan. 'Frank, this is Gaston Duval.'

The two men stared at one another. They were so different that Megan found herself tempted to laugh.

Just as Frank was insignificant, so unobtrusive with his pale skin, his light brown hair, his ordinary unexciting features—so Gaston was the reverse with his lean handsome face, jet-black hair, dark warm eyes and that smile . . . No one could ever overlook Gaston, she thought.

'What's the time?' Megan asked, and when Frank told her, she gasped. 'We *must* go! Miss Tucker doesn't like us to be out too late.'

'And what right has this . . . this Miss Tuck . . . Tucker to say it is time for you to be in bed?' Gaston asked stiffly.

'The headmistress,' Megan said, and laughed. 'Look, say goodbye to Patrick and Georgina for us, Gaston. Come on, Frank.' She took Frank's hand and smiled at Gaston. 'Good-night,' she said.

They walked to the car in silence. Frank only spoke as he drove away.

'So you've fallen, hook, line and sinker,' he said with a strange sadness in his voice.

126

'Oh, Frank, not really, it's just . . .' Megan began.

'I know. Just . . . I don't blame you. I've never met a woman yet who hasn't fallen for that sexy face and that smooth smile,' Frank said bitterly. 'Just imagine being married to him and knowing that he could get any girl he wants just by smiling at her.'

'I'm not thinking of marrying him,' Megan said quickly.

Or had she? she asked herself. If you let yourself love a man like Gaston, you would be jealous, possessive and determined to make him your own . . . You wouldn't be able to help it, she knew.

'Look, this is only the second time I've met him,' she began again as the car shot along the deserted road towards the school, the beams of light showing up the palm trees and the flowering shrubs.

'I imagine the first was enough to do the damage.' Frank looked down at the shadow by his side. 'Just watch out, Meg. You're too sweet a kid to get hurt, and a man like that can really harm you. I wish . . . oh, how I wish you'd never come here,' he said with a sigh.

Megan sat up. 'Frank, that isn't a very nice thing to say. I thought you liked me,' she said accusingly.

His hand covered hers for a moment and then left it.

'That's the trouble, kid,' he said. 'I like you

too much, and I'm darned afraid you're going to get hurt.'

'Oh, Frank, don't worry. I'm not a child.'

'Aren't you?' Frank gave an odd little laugh, 'I'm just wondering what trouble we're getting into tomorrow.'

'It's not as late as that,' she protested. 'It's only three o'clock.'

But three o'clock was unforgivable in Miss Tucker's eyes, as she had no hesitation in telling Megan next day, after sending for her.

'I understand you were not back until three o'clock this morning,' she said, her cheeks red with anger, her eyes cold. 'This is no example to set our young people.'

How had Miss Tucker known? Megan wondered. It could only be Petronella Weston! Had she lain awake all night to check up on her neighbour?

'I'm sorry,' she said sincerely. 'The evening went so fast I had no idea what time it was.'

'You enjoyed the evening?' Miss Tucker spoke as if referring to a den of lions where the Romans tossed the Christians in those distant days.

'Yes. Why . . .'

'I think it was very bad taste on your part, Miss Crane, to go. You are fully aware that your brother and Gaston Duval are two of the most undesirable characters in the town.'

'Miss Tucker!' Megan stood up, so angry she could hardly speak. 'Patrick Crane

128

happens to be my brother. You have no right to say . . .'

Miss Tucker was on her feet, too, her cheeks an even brighter red now.

'I have every right. I'm in charge of these girls and must allow no one of dubious nature near them. Mr Lambert engaged you, and why I cannot think. You should never have been given the job. What he'll say, though, when he hears you went to that party . . .'

'Miss Tucker, he told me to go.' Megan managed to get a word in and Miss Tucker gaped, her mouth falling open.

'He told you to go . . .? He . . .'

'Yes, Miss Tucker. I asked his permission and he said he thought it was a good idea.' With that, Megan walked out. Why should she stand there and be insulted by Miss Tucker? And what right had she to call Patrick an undesirable character?

Megan went back to her flat. In half an hour she had a lesson to give, but until then she would sit on her balcony, basking in the sun, loving the beauty of the deep blue sea, the chatter of the birds. What would happen next? she wondered. Miss Tucker was sure to have a row with Craig Lambert about it. Who would win?

And if Miss Tucker did, was that going to be the end of this life? Megan wondered. Yet how could Miss Tucker win? she thought, feeling suddenly certain. Craig would never let her!

CHAPTER V

Craig Lambert didn't return until the end of the week and Megan was glad when she saw him in the big dining-room.

Miss Tucker had said no more to Megan about her *late night out,* yet Megan knew she must have told many of the staff, for quite a few of them now ignored her completely. Frank Parr, too, had been interviewed by Miss Tucker and lost his temper, telling her she had no right to control his private life and that three a.m. was not such a terrible time.

'At least I brought Miss Crane back!' he had finished angrily, and stormed out of the room.

Now he, like Megan, was waiting for Craig's reaction.

'In a sense,' Frank had said only the day before as they lay in the sunshine on the beach, 'he has to stand up for the headmistress. On the other hand, it's rather Victorian to expect the staff to be in by midnight. After all, these precious girlies are going out into the wicked world in a few years' time, so shouldn't we break it to them gently that adults can stay out after midnight?'

Megan had laughed. 'I just wonder what Mr Lambert will say!' She shook her head. 'I'm afraid he won't like it.' This, though she had not told Frank, was what worried her most.

130

Had she let Craig down? she wondered. He had trusted her enough to let her go to the party; had it, then, been up to her to see that she obeyed the School's rules?

The longer she lived on the island the more she loved it, she had thought, as they walked up to the school. Tiny coloured birds were hovering over the flowers whose fragrant scents drifted on the warm breeze, the palm trees moved gently and the whole atmosphere . . .

She had grown to know many of the girls quite well and she looked forward to her classes. Several of the staff, too, were getting more friendly. Now, if Craig decided she must go . . . So the tension had been great which made her smile, perhaps more warmly than usual, as she glanced down the table. He lifted his hand and smiled as well.

Miss Weston, sitting next to her, snorted.

'You think you can talk him out of it?' she asked, helping herself to another roll.

Startled, Megan turned. 'Talk who out of what?'

Miss Weston looked amused. 'Craig Lambert, of course. You seem able to twist him round your little finger.'

'I don't!' Megan blushed.

'Don't you? It seems you do. You can break the school rules and get away with it.'

'If you mean because Frank and I were late that once . . .'

'Once is enough. You should never have gone to the party.'

Megan drew a deep breath. 'Look, Miss Weston, let's face it. I didn't mean to be late. It was simply that the time went fast. In any case, Mr Lambert said he thought it a good idea if I went to the party . . .'

'There you are!' Miss Weston said triumphantly. 'Just what I said—you can do what you like. None of us could have gone.'

'Please . . .' Megan lowered her voice, for several of the staff were looking down the table at them and it would not be a good welcome to Craig if she was involved in a fight with Petronella Weston in the dining-room! 'I think you forget that Patrick Crane is my brother. That was why Mr Lambert thought I should go.'

Mr Taft, the maths teacher, who rarely spoke, leaned across the table. 'I understand you are a good choreographer, Miss Crane?'

Welcoming the change of subject, Megan looked at his stern face and saw the friendliness in his eyes. 'Yes, I used to do quite a lot in England,' she said.

'Well, we're planning the end-of-the-year concert and I wondered if you would work out the choreography of a dance that could involve the different classes, showing their slow but steady improvement, not only in dancing but in every way.'

'It sounds a marvellous idea!' Megan said

eagerly. 'Could we discuss it?'

'I'll be delighted to,' said Paul Taft. 'We've another month before the end of term. The holidays will give you time to work it all out.'

Petronella Weston stood up noisily, scraping her chair back and calling attention to herself as she left the table.

'What's the matter with her?' asked Megan, startled, aware that both Miss Tucker and Mr Lambert were looking down at them.

Paul Taft, who so rarely laughed, did laugh this time.

'Take no notice of her, Miss Crane. She's suffering from malicious jealousy,' he said quietly across the table. 'Don't let it worry you. Poor Petronella, she can't help it.'

'Help what?' Everyone had begun to start speaking noisily, so Megan felt she could talk across the table without anyone hearing.

The elderly man smiled. 'You haven't noticed? My dear girl, you are very young.' He shook his head. 'Some other time,' he added, as the meal came to a close.

Megan had just finished her last class for the day when the message arrived: *Mr Lambert would like to see you immediately.*

So it had come, Megan thought. Soon she would know the worst. Would she and Frank be asked to leave? Or perhaps she was the one at fault?

She hurried past the girls, but Anarita stopped her for a moment.

133

'Miss Meg, it isn't true, is it?' she asked, her lovely face worried.

'What isn't true, Anarita? Look, Mr Lambert wants to see me.'

'Is he going to sack you?' Anarita looked even more dismayed.

Megan laughed. 'I hope not. What makes you think . . . ?'

'Everyone's talking—they're saying you and Mr Parr are . . . are in love.' Anarita frowned. 'I don't think you are.'

'We are not in love.' Megan patted Anarita's arm. 'Look, Mr Parr and I are good friends— that's all. Now I really must go, Anarita, we mustn't make Mr Lambert cross.'

'He must be to have sent for you. Miss Meg, if he sacks you, we'll all go on strike,' Anarita promised.

Megan laughed. 'Bless you, but that won't be necessary,' she said, and hurried down the corridor.

As she went past a wide open door, the warm fragrant air came in to envelop her and for a moment she paused, looking out at the blue cloudless sky, the beauty of it all. Suppose Craig was going to sack her? Suppose she had to leave this?

Craig? She thought with a shock that these days she always thought of him as *Craig*. Why? He had never told her to use his Christian name. She hardly knew him . . . and yet, in a way, she did know him. And what she knew

134

didn't make sense—it didn't fit in with all Patrick and Gaston had said about Craig Lambert's selfish, brutal ruthlessness.

She knocked on his door and heard a curt, 'Come in!'

Suddenly unsure of herself, even almost certain that she would leave the room without a job, Megan obeyed. Craig was bent over his desk, talking on the phone. He looked up and pointed to a chair, so Megan sat down.

She looked round the room. It was so typically him, she thought. She tried to relax, but could not help feeling worried as she watched his face change as he talked angrily into the phone.

'That's absurd! You had plenty of time. No, I do not agree, and I will not tolerate it. I gave you warning. No, I will not agree.' He put down the receiver and looked at the slight girl looking so terrified as she sat in the chair, her hands tightly clenched.

'Well,' he began with a smile, 'I hear you enjoyed the party so much that you forgot the time. Parr was an equal sinner, of course.'

'It wasn't so much that I enjoyed it,' Megan tried to explain. 'We didn't get there very early and there was food to eat and then Patrick danced with me . . . well, time must have flown. Then he and Georgina danced and we all watched and that took quite a while. When Frank . . . I mean, Mr Parr told me the time, I was really shocked.'

135

'So was he, I gather,' Craig said with a chuckle. 'I must congratulate you on persuading Frank Parr to go. He's always rather worried me. What I call a loner. You seem to get on well?'

'Oh yes, we do. He's great fun and—well . . . Megan paused.

'You don't find much friendship from the rest of the staff?'

'In a way, yes. Mr Taft is awfully nice and so is Herta Bauer, the German mistress, and Aline Delaine. I get on all right with them, but . . . and the accompanists are very friendly, too.'

'Mr Taft was telling me he has asked you to choreograph the dancing for our next school concert. He said you were interested?'

Megan nodded. She was feeling more relaxed. 'His idea was a good one. But . . .' She hesitated as she looked at Craig Lambert. 'I really am sorry about being late that night, Mr Lambert. We didn't mean to be.'

'I'm aware of that,' Craig almost clipped the words impatiently.

'I'm afraid Miss Tucker was very angry.'

'So I gather.' A smile curled round his mouth. 'I also gather you stormed out in a temper.'

'Yes, I'm afraid I did, but she said something very nasty about Patrick and he is, after all, my brother,' Megan said, leaning forward, her hands twisting together again. 'I

136

mean, no matter what you or she may think of him, I'm not going to stand by and let you . . .'

'I quite agree. Family loyalty is a natural thing,' Craig acknowledged. 'Well, that's all, I think. I wanted to see you to ask you to co-operate with Mr Taft. He always organises our concerts and I think you'll find him very pleasant to work with.' He stood up and Megan did, too.

She felt stunned a little. 'That's all? You're not angry with me?'

'Should I be?' he asked, coming round the desk towards her. 'What crime did you commit? You went to your brother's dance with my approval. Naturally you couldn't walk out in the middle, but I understand you left almost as soon as the exhibition dancing was over.'

'Yes, we did.' Bless Frank, Megan was thinking, for he obviously hadn't mentioned Gaston Duval!

They walked to the door and as he opened it, Craig looked at her gravely. 'Just one thing, Miss Crane. This is for your own good and has nothing to do with the School, but I would ask you to be on your guard. Gaston Duval has a way with women, particularly romantic-minded girls.' He closed the door before she could answer. She stood still for a moment and then went up to her flat. Craig had been on her side, after all. He had understood and trusted her. But why must everyone warn her

137

about Gaston? She had only met him twice and was unlikely ever to meet him again.

She stood out on her balcony and stared at the sea as she suddenly realised that everything was all right, and she had not been sacked. She was so glad she wanted to dance and sing . . . she had known she wanted to stay at Lambert School, but it wasn't until now, when she knew she was staying, that she realised how much it meant to her.

Not only the beauty of the island, not only the friendliness of the girls she taught, and the sweet old men who played the piano for the dancing lessons; not only for Frank and his jokes and big-brother attitude, nor for the German and French women who were helping her with her languages, but it was something more.

This was her home.

It sounded ridiculous. She hadn't been with them a whole term yet—and it still felt like home. This was her dream land, the dream she had had as a child whenever she was unhappy; a land of palm trees and huge roaring waves dancing against the coral reefs, and the voices of the locals singing and laughing, the chatter of the monkeys, the sweet song of the birds . . . this was her home. She felt she never wanted to leave it, never to return to England and Hastings which seemed a thousand million light years away . . .

She was staying! That was all that mattered.

As the days passed, they slipped back into the old routines, with Megan's lessons changing as she tested each class to find what kind of dancing they enjoyed most. She had long talks with Mr Taft about it and he agreed that that was good.

'Not what they do the best,' Megan said gravely, 'but what they enjoy doing most—that way they'll express themselves.'

He nodded, 'An excellent idea.'

Some of the staff had dropped their icy disapproval, Megan's French and German lessons continued, but Miss Weston ignored Megan whenever she could. One day, Megan talked to Mr Taft as they sat on the terrace at the back, slightly above the tennis courts. He had a sheet of paper before him as they planned the number of dancers they could have for each session, for there had to be sufficient room to move them off.

'Mr Taft, why did you say Miss Weston couldn't *help* it?' Megan asked suddenly, looking at the elderly man by her side, his dark hair slightly grey. 'You wouldn't tell me at the time, but she's so very unfriendly. Did I offend her in some way?'

His grave face relaxed. 'It was not your fault, my dear. You are young and attractive.'

'But so is Petronella Weston. I think she's

139

beautiful, and that husky voice . . .'

'I agree, but it's no competition against a twenty-year-old with an innocent, fey little frightened face.'

'Is that me?' Megan was startled. 'Do I look fey and frightened?'

'Sometimes.' His eyes twinkled. 'Not to worry, it adds to your charm. Now, let's return to our work.'

'No, Mr Taft,' Megan pretended to be stern, smiling at the same time as she looked at him. 'You haven't told me *why* you were sorry for her.'

'Surely,' he said slowly. 'You can see that she, like all the female staff, is in love with Craig Lambert.'

'In love with Craig?' Megan repeated slowly. 'I hadn't realised it.'

'You walk as in a dream, my dear.' Gently he put his hand under her chin, tilting up her head so that he could look in her eyes. 'Are you sure you're not in love with him yourself?'

Megan was startled. 'Of course not! Why, I've hardly known him any time.'

'Love doesn't take *any time,*' Paul Taft said with a smile. 'Now if we could concentrate on this work . . .'

'Yes, Mr Taft,' Megan said meekly, but although she listened to what he said, his voice seemed to be coming from far away, nor could she concentrate on what she had to suggest for she found his words going over and over again

140

in her mind.

'*Are you sure you're not in love with him yourself?*'

In love—with Craig Lambert?

It was ridiculous, she told herself. Of course she wasn't. Yet she had noticed how different a room felt when Craig walked in. He had started a habit of looking in at the dancing classes, asking questions, and watching the girls, and the whole atmosphere of the room seemed to change immediately. Was that love?

It couldn't possibly be, she decided. She liked him, indeed she liked him very much, for he had stood on her side, trusting her, and although there was this old family feud with the Duvals, in which Patrick seemed involved in some way, Craig had not allowed it to influence his opinion of her.

That was all it was, she decided, and when later that day, dancing with the girls on their social evening, Anarita said:

'Is it true everyone is in love with Mr Lambert?'

'How would I know?' Megan could answer with an innocent smile.

Anarita tucked her hand through Megan's arm. 'Are you?'

Megan laughed. 'Of course I'm not. I admire him, that's all.'

'But you must be in love with someone,' Anarita persisted. 'I mean no girl can really live unless she loves someone.'

'Well, I seem to be living very well. So do you, Anarita,' Megan teased.

The lovely Italian-English girl looked thoughtful.

'Do I? Yet I feel unfinished. I don't feel a real me, if you know what I mean. I just can't wait to be married. It will be so . . . such a happening. Have you ever been in love?'

Megan thought. 'No, actually I haven't. I never had a real boy-friend because of my father, and . . .'

'Do you mind? I mean never having had a boy-friend? Don't you feel sort of . . . well, as if you're not a real woman yet?'

Megan laughed. 'Look, Anarita, there are millions of perfectly happy women who have never had nor ever want to have a boy-friend. That doesn't mean they're not real women. Some of us love and some of us don't.'

'Well,' Anarita sighed, 'I don't think you're the kind who don't . . . I know I'm not.'

'Good grief!' exclaimed Frank Parr, slightly limping as he joined them. 'I've just broken my glasses. I'll have to go in tomorrow to get new ones. Want a lift in, Meg?'

'Thanks,' Megan smiled.

'Can I come, too, Mr Parr?' Anarita asked quickly.

He looked enquiringly at Megan. Megan had been rather worried recently because every time she and Anarita went into town, Anarita got lost. Or rather, she lost Anarita, and when she found her, Anarita always accused Megan of being the one who got lost. This had been going on for some time, but lately, Anarita had been 'lost' for longer intervals.

'Look, Anarita,' Megan said slowly, 'I know you may think it's a great joke, but you are my responsibility and I don't like the way you vanish.'

Anarita pouted, 'I don't mean to.'

'Don't you? I sometimes wonder if you do. I don't find it funny at all.'

'So if we take you, Anarita,' Frank chimed in, 'it's understood you don't get lost. Right?'

She looked at him. 'Is it my fault if Miss Crane gets lost? I have to look for her, don't I?'

'Let's cut out that blarney stuff. You promise not to get lost?' Frank Parr demanded.

Anarita shrugged. 'I promise to try and not let Miss Crane get lost.'

'All right. One more chance,' said Frank. Later he talked to Megan about it.

'That girl has changed a lot in the last weeks,' he said.

Megan smiled, thinking what a beautiful warm night it was with stars sparkling in the dark sky as she and Frank stood just outside on the terrace.

'Has she?'

'Is it your influence, Meg?' he asked,

looking down at her.

'I can't see what I've done to help,' Megan began.

'You've made her feel that someone cares,' a deep voice interrupted.

Both Megan and Frank were startled as Craig came through the open French doors.

'I apologise for overhearing what you were talking about,' Craig Lambert said, 'but your voices came in clear. I think it's Miss Crane who has helped Anarita, Parr. She was a difficult child from the day she came here. Do you think she's mixing better with fellow students? She's not depending on Miss Crane too much?'

'I don't think so,' Frank said quickly. 'She rarely has a tantrum these days—remember how she went on hunger-strike, once, because she failed her exams?' he chuckled. 'She was a real handful. I must say I notice a big difference in her. The deliberate cheekiness that was a form of rebellion has also vanished.'

'Yes,' Craig agreed. 'I think we can thank Miss Crane for that,' he said, and went back into the school.

Frank whistled softly. 'You are in favour, Meg,' he said quietly. 'He's right, too. You've done Anarita a world of good.'

'I'm glad if I have helped. I'm very fond of her and yet at times she puzzles me. It's as if she's laughing at me, as if . . . well, as if she's triumphant about something or other, somewhere she has got the better of me.'

'It all sounds very complicated,' Frank laughed. 'We'd better go in or Miss Tucker's tongue will begin to quiver. Has she said anything more to you about our night out?'

'No. She hardly ever talks to me except to do with some extracurricular work.'

They went inside the school. The dance hall was empty, but the record was still playing. Frank turned to Megan.

'Meg, if you don't want to then say so, but I'd like to try to dance. I've . . . well, maybe it was cowardice on my part or pride, but I used to love dancing. I wonder if my foot would be the handicap I thought it.'

'Of course I'll dance with you, Frank. Let's start the tune again.' Megan ran across to the record player. 'What would you like? Modern or an old-fashioned waltz?' She laughed. 'The choice is yours.'

'What about a nice romantic tango?'

'Okay,' Megan called, putting on the record.

As the music began, Frank limped across the room, holding out his arms.

'Oh, my love . . .' he chanted. 'My dear and sweet love, come into my arms, my dear one . . .'

He put his arm round her and took her hand . . . and they danced. Frank's first steps were clumsy, but that, Megan knew, was from nervousness. As the music went on, his self-confidence returned and his lameness was hardly noticeable.

As the music came to an end, Frank stopped, his arm still round Megan. He leant forward and kissed her gently.

'Thank you.'

'It was . . .' Megan began, but the words died in her mouth, for she saw over Frank's shoulder that in the doorway stood Miss Tucker, her cheeks bright red, her eyes flashing, her hand on Craig Lambert's arm. He was looking at them gravely, his eyebrows drawn together.

'You see, I told you! That's why I fetched you. When I saw how they were behaving!' Miss Tucker began. 'You wouldn't believe me . . .'

Frank swung round, releasing Megan. He held out his hands expressively. 'Just think what a fool I've been all these years, Miss Tucker. I thought I couldn't dance, but Megan has shown me I can. I feel I'm reborn.' He laughed. 'If you knew what it means to me, to be able to dance! Well, Miss Tucker,' he went on cheerfully, 'at least now your girls will have another male partner to show them how it goes.'

*   *   *

As Frank drove them into the small town next day, Anarita chattered away happily while

146

Megan found herself thinking of the day before and Miss Tucker's startled, almost disappointed voice as she heard what Frank had said, and Craig Lambert had walked across the floor, smiling approvingly. Poor Miss Tucker—she had looked so squashed as she almost hastened away.

'Miss Crane seems to be quite useful round here,' Craig had observed with a friendly smile, and Frank had nodded.

'We needed some young blood, I think,' he had said.

It was then that Craig had surprised them both as he looked grave. 'I think you're right. That's been my opinion for some time, but . . .' He had laughed. 'Well, I'm glad about the dancing, Parr. Why not practise a bit while you've got the chance?' and he had walked out, leaving them alone.

Frank had whistled softly. 'He is in a good mood, Meg, my dear! Looks like you're working a miracle.'

Which was absurd, of course, Megan was thinking as she sat in the back of the car because, for a treat, Frank had let Anarita sit in front. Despite the girl's seventeen years, Megan was thinking, Anarita was very young in some respects, and now as she sat sideways, looking at Frank, her legs curled up under her, she seemed unable to stop talking.

As the town came in sight, Frank arranged where to meet them.

'We could have a cup of coffee or something cold before we go back.'

'I promise I won't let her out of my sight,' Anarita said with a laugh, tucking her hand through Megan's arm. 'So don't try to run away, Miss Meg.'

They all laughed as they stood near the market, which was their usual meeting-place. It was bright and noisy, with all the gay colours and women chattering; huge baskets of fruit and food and small children running round and playing.

Frank walked off to see about his glasses and Megan led the way down the crowded street. It was certainly much slower with the two of them walking arm in arm, but she decided to say nothing, as Anarita must not go off on her own. Not that any harm could come to her, Megan was certain of that, but she felt responsible to Craig; he trusted her and surely that meant she should be loyal to him?

On the other side of the street, she suddenly saw Tracy Thompson. He waved his hand and Anarita was pushed back a little, so Megan didn't see if she waved to the hippie-artist, as they called Tracy, but Megan, who quite liked him and couldn't understand Anarita's contempt for him, lifted her hand and smiled.

Strolling past the shops, discussing clothes and what the next fashion would be, Megan caught her breath with dismay as she saw walking towards them, a familiar figure.

148

Gaston Duval!

Oh no! she thought. Craig would never forgive her if Gaston stopped to speak to them and she had to introduce Anarita. Craig, like Miss Tucker, had a poor opinion of Gaston for some unknown reason, and it would be a wonderful weapon for Miss Tucker to use if she could say that Megan Crane was introducing the pupils to undesirable characters. Megan could almost hear Miss Tucker speaking.

Hastily she looked around. They were close to a bazaar.

'Let's go in here,' she said quickly, turning to the girl by her side. 'I want to look at some bracelets. I've got to get one for a present.'

Anarita followed her into the shop. It was crowded and Megan went to the far end, pretending to be interested in the bracelets on display. She hated telling lies, but anything was permissible if she was to do what Craig expected of her.

'Do look at this, Anarita,' she said, and wondered why her voice was so shrill.

Was she nervous? Frightened of Craig's anger? she asked herself. It wasn't that, she knew very well. But she appreciated the fact that he trusted her, that he relied on her to keep her side of it. And introducing an attractive man like Gaston to a romantic-minded teenager was surely not a good idea?

The shop began to empty a little and

149

Megan, glancing down the narrow aisle that divided the two counters, could plainly see the doorway. And Gaston Duval stood there! Waiting?

She looked round and saw that Anarita was staring at a long black and white beaded necklet.

'That's pretty. Are you going to buy it?' she asked, fumbling in her handbag for her purse and hastily looking for the cheapest bracelet she could see. 'It's awfully hot in here, Anarita, makes me feel I can't breathe. Would you buy that bracelet for me? I'll wait outside.'

If Anarita was surprised she didn't show it. She took the money and waited patiently for the two assistants to get through their many customers and get to her.

Meanwhile, Megan had hurried outside to speak to Gaston.

'Look,' she began, 'I'm sorry about this, Mr Duval, but the school is very strict about allowing the girls to come into town, and . . .'

He smiled. 'And they mustn't meet undesirables? It is so? Ah,' he laughed, 'it is old-fashioned, that school, is it not? You wish me to take no notice of you? But that would be rude.'

'Hullo, Gaston . . nice to see you again.' Anarita's loud voice seemed to pierce Megan's head as she turned and saw the girl, so lovely, so young and so vulnerable in her white sheaf dress, smiling at Gaston.

150

Gaston bowed. 'Ah, it is Anarita Marco! But you have grown, my child. You were so young . . .'

Anarita laughed. 'The years have gone.' She turned to Megan. 'Why didn't you tell me Gaston Duval was visiting the island?'

'I didn't know you knew him,' Megan said weakly.

'Of course I know him.' Anarita laughed with some contempt. 'Everyone in Europe knows Gaston Duval. Isn't that true?' she asked, tilting her head, her long black hair swinging.

He smiled at her, his eyes narrowed. 'I am flattered by your remark, Anarita.' He bowed. 'Time has worked a miracle. You were a fat child with untidy hair, and now . . .' He gave another little bow, his face crinkling into a smile. 'Words could not describe your beauty.'

Anarita laughed. 'I am flattered by *your* remark, Gaston. I got the bracelet you wanted, Miss Crane.'

Gaston lifted his hand. 'Ah, but I am not right in the head. I was looking for Miss Crane as I have a message. He turned to Megan. 'It is from your brother. His wife is ill . . .'

'Oh no! I am sorry.'

'It is not serious, so do not feel disturbed, but they would like to see you. I think Patrick needs your help. Georgina is being—how do you call it?--difficult? She will not listen to him, she says she is very ill, but of course, that

151

is nonsense. She is just being . . .' Gaston smiled at them both, a quick intimate smile that seemed to imply that he thought the girl he looked at was the most beautiful in the world, Megan was thinking, crossing her fingers and hoping Anarita would not fall for Gaston's French charm. 'Perhaps if you had a talk with her? We could go now?'

'Oh no, we couldn't,' Megan said quickly. That would be the last straw in Miss Tucker's eyes, she knew. 'I've got to go back to School now, but I'll come in later. I can always get a lift.'

'That is good, yes? I can drive you back,' Gaston promised.

'Thank you.' Megan took hold of Anarita's arm. 'We must go. We can't keep Mr Parr waiting.'

'Why not?' Anarita asked. 'He often keeps us waiting.'

Gaston laughed. 'Ah, but I can see, Anarita *chérie,* you have not changed much.' He bowed to them both and walked down the street, immediately merging into the crowd.

'Anarita, where did you meet Mr Duval?' Megan asked as they made their way down towards the market.

'Four years ago in Rome,' Anarita gave a little skip. 'I was thirteen then and longing to fall in love. I was staying with my father's aunt. She is the Contessa Marco and a real socialite. Of course I adored Gaston, he was so romantic. He hardly noticed me, but I didn't mind that. I knew that one day he would.' She laughed happily. 'Isn't he absolutely gorgeous?'

'He's very attractive,' Megan agreed reluctantly, thinking that these visits to the small town might have to stop, for whatever happened, Anarita must not be encouraged to fall in love with the handsome Gaston Duval. Not even Craig would be able to forgive Megan for that, Megan was thinking as they hurried to meet Frank.

'We met Gaston Duval!' Anarita said triumphantly as Frank came, slightly limping, towards them.

'You did what?' The shocked horror on Frank's face merely intensified Megan's dismay. 'Let's have a coffee.'

Sitting down under the gay red and yellow sunshade, they drank their coffee and Anarita told Frank excitedly how she had met Gaston four years ago.

'He didn't even see me, but today he did, didn't he, Miss Crane?' Anarita turned eagerly to the silent Megan. 'You could see that from his eyes. He thought me terrific . . .'

'I imagine he makes every female think that,' Frank said drily.

Anarita laughed. 'You're just jealous, Mr Parr. I bet you'd like to be as handsome as that.'

Megan remembered something and hastily

interrupted Anarita's teasing. 'Georgina, my sister-in-law, is ill, and Patrick wants me to go and see her. I wondered if you'd bring me back after we've taken Anarita back to the school.'

Frank frowned. 'Look, we'll drop you off after this, then I'll take Anarita back and I'll come and fetch you in, say, three hours' time. Right?'

'Frank, that would be wonderful,' Megan began, but Anarita was laughing.

'You're afraid of Gaston Duval, Miss Crane? He offered to drive you back. Wouldn't you rather have him than Mr Parr?'

Megan felt a tremor of anger go through her. 'There's no need to be cheeky, Anarita. You're old enough to know better. Mr Parr is my friend and naturally I'd prefer to come back with him.'

Anarita chuckled. 'I just don't believe you. I bet Gaston's got a white sports car and never drives at less than a hundred miles an hour . . .'

'In that case,' Megan said, finishing her coffee, 'I'm very glad Mr Parr is fetching me.'

Frank promised to explain why Megan would not be at the school for dinner. 'I'll see Miss Tucker,' he said, looking significantly at Megan, and she smiled back gratefully, knowing he would tell Miss Tucker that Anarita had met Gaston Duval at her great-aunt's castle near Rome and that it had nothing to do with Miss Crane!

But would Miss Tucker believe him? Megan

worried silently. She could just hear Anarita's gay triumphant voice as she told her friends about the handsome Frenchman who had told her she was too beautiful for words to describe!

Anarita was certainly in a happy mood, Megan thought miserably, for she herself was not. Now Anarita was teasing Frank again.

'Do you honestly think I should drive back to school alone with you, Mr Parr?' Anarita asked, her eyes dancing. 'Won't Miss Tucker be shocked? Aren't you afraid you might lose your job? Don't you think it's daft, Miss Crane?' She twisted round to look at Megan in the back of the car. 'I'm seventeen, yet at this miserable school I can't even have a boy-friend.'

'Your misfortune, Anarita, is your money,' Frank said drily. 'Your guardian is terrified you'll marry someone after your money.'

'Lovely, I must say!' Anarita replied sarcastically. 'Of course you're right, but it makes one mad, all the same. Anyone would think I was hideous or something if all the men think of is my money.'

Frank turned and smiled at her. 'Never mind, Anarita. You'll soon be twenty-one.'

'Soon,' she said bitterly. 'Four miserable wasted years.'

Frank stopped the car outside the Crane Dancing Studio.

'This is your brother's?' Anarita asked

155

eagerly. 'It looks super: Maybe you'll take me there one day?'

Megan hurriedly got out of the car. 'Maybe,' she said, and added silently, Maybe not! Somehow she couldn't see Craig agreeing to that. She only dreaded the thought of what his reaction was going to be when he heard about Gaston Duval. 'Thanks a ton, Frank,' she said, and he smiled at her understandingly.

' 'Bye!' Anarita called gaily as the car drove away.

Megan felt quite sorry for Frank, for Anarita in a gay mood could be rather irritating after a while.

Megan rang the dangling bell. A Creole girl in a flaming red dress let her in and showed her through to Patrick's small office.

He was writing a letter and looked up. 'Hi, so Gaston found you?' He grinned. 'Hope it didn't embarrass you too much—you had the girl with you, I hear.'

Megan went to stand by his desk. 'How did you know?'

Patrick laughed. 'I have my spies, as well as Lambert School. Seriously, though, I want you to tackle Georgina. She's being positively grotty. She's made up her mind she's ill and though the doctor says she isn't, she says he doesn't know what he's talking about. I've got to get her well.' His face had lost its softness as his mouth hardened. 'I've simply got to, Meg.'

He stood up and took her into the lounge,

pouring her a cold drink and preparing one for himself.

'Do sit down,' he said irritably, and straddled a chair near her. 'Look, talk some sense into Georgina's brain, Meg, or . . .' He sighed. 'We've got to give an exhibition dance on Saturday. Now this isn't just an ordinary Saturday night. By a stroke of luck, I managed to contact one of the biggest blokes in the business and invited him for the weekend. If he likes us—our dancing, I mean—it could open up a new world for us.'

He began to walk about the room impatiently, striking one fist against the palm of his other hand.

'I'm fed up to the teeth, Meg. Fed up with Gaston's wonderful ideas. He has wonderful ideas, I'll grant that, but they just seem to shrivel up. I didn't realise what we'd be up against here. That . . . that Craig Lambert would be too wealthy, too powerful with his influence for us to succeed in fighting. If only Gaston would accept that—but as you probably know, it's more involved because of a family feud that goes back several generations. Absolute tripe!'

Patrick went to stand by the window, his fingers restlessly pleating the white silk curtain.

'I wish I knew why Craig Lambert has this thing about us. It just isn't fair. All Gaston and I have done is to bring money into the island,

157

getting people to invest it here, even come and live here, because it's a pretty ideal life. I just can't understand Lambert, Meg. It wouldn't affect his school. All Gaston and I want is to make it a perfect holiday resort. Lambert doesn't seem to realise—or maybe I should say, doesn't *want* to realise—that it would bring more and better paid jobs for the locals and a much better future because better schools and hospitals could be built, too. The sky's the limit, sort of thing. Craig Lambert is so darned greedy he wants it all his way. I bet he's making a fortune out of that school. Apart from anything else, there's a lot of land here that no one is using. That could be built on, but he won't sell it to us.'

'So you feel you want to get out of the island?' Megan asked.

Patrick swung round. 'I must. It's driving me round the bend, like banging your head against a brick wall. If it wasn't for that lousy school . . .'

'It's a famous school, going for a long time.'

'Time it was closed, it's hopelessly out of date. I know the millionaires like to send their little girls there, but I wonder if it's as safe as they believe.' Patrick was scowling.

'I think that's why Mr Lambert doesn't like all this . . . well, this publicity and tourists coming, Patrick. It used to be a quiet island on which a stranger was instantly recognised.'

'Well, let him find another island where

158

there's no one and rebuild the school. Why aren't we allowed to make money as well as him?'

Megan stood up. 'Maybe I should see Georgina, though I can't think how I can help, because she . . . well, I don't think she's ever liked me.'

'Georgina likes only one person,' Patrick said bitterly as he led the way down the corridor towards the bedroom. '*Georgina Crane,* and that's the truth.'

Megan went into the luxuriously furnished room rather reluctantly, for she and Georgina had never been friends, nor could Megan forget, looking at the wide double bed, the heavy rose-coloured silk curtains, the beautiful dressing table, that it had all been bought with the money Patrick got from his father; money she and their father had sent him, sacrificing many things they needed.

Georgina smiled weakly. 'Patrick asked you to talk sense into me?' she asked.

She was propped up by pillows, but Megan was shocked to see the difference in her face from the beautiful if hard face it normally was. Now she looked pale, her skin taut.

'What's wrong?' she asked.

'The doctor said nothing. He should have the pain I've got!' Georgina lightly touched her stomach. 'Gastroenteritis, I think they call it. I think it was food poisoning. I feel like . . . well, ghastly, and all Pat can do is talk about

159

Saturday night. That means more to him than I do.'

'He seems unhappy here.'

'Unhappy! Your brother is unhappy anywhere. If your dad hadn't spoiled him . . .' Georgina said bitterly. Her usually beautiful crown of dark hair was limp and lifeless, hanging round her pale tired face. 'Pat expects everything to be handed to him. He can't see you have to work for it. He should have been born with a fairy's wand—or is it Dick Whittington's magic lamp? I always get confused.' She laughed. 'I'm sorry, Meg, but Patrick is just a spoiled brat, and as for Gaston . . . that man can squeeze money out of an empty turtle shell. Watch out—for your money.'

'Money?' Megan said slowly, looking at the pale face before her. Now wasn't the right time, she decided, to be truthful. Money—what hope had she or her father ever had to have money when Patrick was always in need? In need . . . Megan looking round, wondered what her father's reaction would be if he could see this house and the dancing studio. 'No, I've only got my salary. Look, Georgina, you may feel all right on Saturday. This sort of thing can go quite quickly, sometimes.'

'Sometimes,' Georgina echoed. 'Look, Megan, I gather you and Craig Lambert get on well. Everyone's surprised. I don't know how you do it, because from what I hear, he's

160

absolutely the end.'

'He's very nice,' Megan said quickly. 'Understanding and tolerant. He's . . . well, I just don't understand why people say such things about him.'

'Maybe he's different with you. Look, Meg, I love this island and this way of living and I don't want to go. Couldn't you talk this *very nice, understanding, tolerant* Craig Lambert into seeing some sense?' she asked, sarcastically repeating Megan's own words. 'All we want is to make some money. I'm fed up to the teeth with debts piling up. If Craig Lambert would only be sensible.'

Patrick opened the door and came in. 'Visitor to meet you, Meg, so come along.' He hardly looked at his wife and she was gazing thoughtfully at her fingernails, Megan noticed, as she said good-bye and followed her brother to the lounge.

He bent and whispered in her ear, 'Gaston's mother. She's the one with all the lolly, so be nice to her.'

Before Megan could reply, he was opening the door.

'Here she is . . .' he said gaily. 'Madame Duval, this is my sister Megan.'

Gaston Duval's mother? Megan was thinking as she followed him.

A small slight woman with snow-white hair stood up. She had Gaston's dark eyes, and his smile.

'I have wanted to meet you,' she said. 'Do sit down.'

Megan obeyed and they sat for a moment, just looking at one another. Mrs Duval—or Madame Duval, for that was what Patrick had called her before he left them—was a beautiful woman, Megan thought, simply but elegantly dressed in an amber-coloured silk suit.

'Yes,' Madame Duval said thoughtfully. 'I can see what Gaston means.'

'What he means?' Megan echoed. 'I . . .'

Madame Duval smiled. 'You know, of course, that he wishes to marry you.'

'Gaston?' Megan's surprise resounded in her voice as well as in the name. 'I had no idea. He's . . . I mean, we hardly know one another.'

Madame Duval smiled. 'Is that so essential when you are young? You find him attractive?'

Megan blushed. 'He's very . .

'Smooth is perhaps the best word,' Madame Duval who was obviously English, chuckled. 'Ah, he can't help it. Women always collapse when he smiles at them. He has been in and out of love for many years. That's why I was so happy when he wrote and told me he wanted to marry an English girl. I came from Devonshire a very long time ago.' She laughed again. 'So—I thought—Gaston at last is ready to settle down. That is why I came at once.'

'But . . . but please,' Megan leaned forward. 'Please, I think Gaston must have been joking. We've only met once or twice and . . . well . . .'

She felt confused as well as surprised.

'I know when my son is joking,' Madame Duval's voice changed a little. 'He's like your brother. It's not always wise to have such wealthy parents. It spoils them. They expect to have everything on a silver platter and when it doesn't come, they're indignant, they feel they've been cheated. I know it so well . . .'

Madame Duval's voice seemed to be coming from far away to Megan, for she was trying to grasp one thing. Madame Duval had said: 'He is like your brother,' meaning Gaston was like Patrick because 'it is not always wise to have such wealthy parents'. What did she mean? Patrick hadn't wealthy parents. Did Madame Duval think that the Cranes were wealthy?

She realised that Madame Duval was still talking, and with an effort she concentrated on what the old lady was saying:

'I find it so amusing, you know. This family feud, I thought it was only in legends that it happened, yet it is true. When Gaston insisted on coming here, I tried to argue with him. It would be hopeless, I said, you cannot win in a battle with a man like Craig Lambert.'

Megan's limbs seemed to stiffen, but Madame Duval did not notice as she went on:

'I expect you know that Craig Lambert's grand-father was in love with a beautiful girl, but my father-in-law married her. I never knew her, but judging from the portraits I've seen

163

she was very lovely indeed. Anyhow, this started a most foolish sort of feud. Everything my father-in-law did, old Mr Lambert did his best to ruin. It was the same when we lived here, but my husband was more clever.' She chuckled. 'Or perhaps the luck of the Duvals had changed, for Craig Lambert's father had one great weakness. He was a gambler. My husband always won. That is how we got so much land here on the island. So when my son declared that he wanted to make this a holiday island I knew why. Gaston loved his father—they would talk for hours about the Lamberts. So,' she laughed, 'I understood. But I knew it would be no good. Craig Lambert has brains and he is not a gambler. He has no weakness. He is tough. Ruthless,' she said thoughtfully, her eyes watching Megan.

'I don't think he is that,' Megan said quickly. 'He has the reputation of the school to consider, you know. The school means a lot to him.'

'I'm not surprised—the money it must bring in.'

'I don't think it's only the money . . .' Megan began, but stopped as she saw Madame Duval smile.

'Ah, I see that Gaston has a rival,' said Madame Duval. 'You *are* in love with Craig Lambert?'

Megan tried to will her cheeks from going red as she clenched her hands and made

164

herself smile. 'I admire him in many ways, but that isn't love.'

'But he loves you? That's true, isn't it?' Madame Duval put her hands up to her snow-white hair and patted it. 'Gaston told me so. Everyone knows that Craig Lambert is in love with you and that you can do nothing wrong.'

Megan's face now was bright red, judging from the way her cheeks burned.

'That's not true! Mr Lambert isn't . . .' she began, but Madame Duval laughed.

'You're so innocent—or appear so, my dear. You didn't know Gaston loved you and now you declare that Craig Lambert doesn't. It is the old feud again—a Lambert versus a Duval. I wonder who will win this time.' She looked at her watch. 'I must go. I have an invitation for dinner.' She held out her hand and took hold of Megan's. 'I am glad we have met. I think I shall like you as my daughter-in-law.'

'But please . . .' Megan tried to speak, but Madame Duval was on her feet, opening the door, just turning with a last smile.

'That is, of course, if Gaston wins.'

And then she was gone. Megan hurried to the window and saw a waiting car with a chauffeur standing ready.

She sat down on the couch, her legs suddenly weak. What did it all mean? Was Gaston in love with her or had he pretended it in the hope of pleasing his mother and perhaps getting more money? Patrick must have lied about his family and led the Duvals to believe that the Cranes were wealthy people. But what really worried Megan was *who* had started the rumour that Craig Lambert was in love with her? How absolutely awful if Craig got to hear of it.

It was a relief when Frank arrived and Megan gave a hasty goodbye to Patrick, then looked in on Georgina and found her asleep, before hurrying out to Frank.

They had just left the town behind when Frank said:

'What's wrong?'

'Just about everything,' Megan admitted. 'How did you get on?'

'I couldn't find Miss Tucker, so I got Lambert. I explained the situation and he quite understood.'

'You mean he wasn't mad about it? Did you tell him about Gaston Duval?'

Frank chuckled. 'Of course. The whole school knew within half an hour. I guessed Anarita would have a whale of a time talking, so I got in first. I told Lambert the truth, the simple truth—that you did your best to prevent Anarita from meeting Duval but that Anarita had already met him at her aunt's home in Rome, so he couldn't be mad at you about that, could he?'

Megan smiled her gratitude. 'He may not want her to come in so often, though.'

'That's a point.' Frank jammed on the brake

166

and then apologised. 'Those damn goats! Nearly hit one of them. On the other hand, Meg, I don't think Gaston Duval is Anarita's cup of tea.'

'You don't?'

Megan had not been able to hide her surprise and she saw an odd smile on Frank's lips.

'No, he's more the type girls of your age go for. Sure you're not interested?'

'No. I do find him rather . . . well . . .'

Frank chuckled, 'I know.'

'Frank, I'm worried about something,' she confessed.

'I knew it. Weep on my shoulder, then.'

'No, it's not like that, but . . . Look, Madame Duval . . . Gaston's mother was there. She's awfully nice—English, born in Devon but lived on the Continent most of her life. She said some rather odd things.'

'Such as?' Frank drove carefully as they turned a blind corner. It was a dark night, the stars brightening the sky, but for once clouds had closed over the moon.

'Well, I think it sounds absolutely mad, but . . . but she said Gaston Duval wants to marry me.'

'*What?*' The car swerved and Frank was occupied for a moment straightening it. 'Sorry about that, but it was a shock. I didn't know you knew him that well.'

'I don't—that's the point. I've only met

him—I think three times. I'm wondering . . .'
Megan paused. Should she be confiding in
Frank? she wondered. Or was he on Craig's
side? So what, if he was? Wasn't she? She felt
confused, her head aching. 'Look, Frank,
we've never been alone together. I mean, he's
never . . .'

'Chatted you up?'

She laughed. 'Of course he hasn't. I hardly
know him. It seems that Madame Duval has all
the money and she's eager for him to settle
down, so I'm wondering if Gaston said it to . . .'

'Reassure her?'

'Yes, I suppose one could call it that.
Anyhow, she came to the island on purpose to
meet me and she seemed to think I would do.'

'Well, that's nice, I must say. Very, very
nice,' Frank said drily. 'And how do you feel
about it?'

'I think it's absolute . . .' Megan gave a little
laugh. 'Look, Frank, it's daft. I don't even
know him.'

'But you find him attractive?'

'What if I do? You don't want to marry
every man you find attractive.'

They could see the school in the distance.

'But, Frank,' Megan said almost
desperately, 'that's not the end of it. She also
said rumour had it that Craig wants to marry
me. She said it was quite a joke, like a
repetition of the reason for the old feud and
she wondered who would be the winner.'

Frank had slowed down as he drove into the school grounds.

'And how do you feel about that?' he asked, his voice suddenly hoarse. 'Has Lambert . . . ?'

'Of course he hasn't. That's just it, Frank. Suppose he hears the gossip?'

Frank stopped the car and turned to look at her. The light from the big house made it possible to see each other's faces.

'You haven't answered my question. How do you feel about that? I mean, marrying Lambert? Supposing he did ask you?'

'Well,' Megan took a deep breath, 'it isn't likely to happen. Please don't tell anyone, Frank.'

'You can trust me.'

'The awful part is . . . suppose he hears the rumour and thinks . . . ?'

Frank laughed. 'That you started it? Could be, of course. Even if he didn't, I can bet on quite a few of the staff who would accuse you of it.'

He got out of the car and opened the car door for her.

'Don't worry, Meg,' he said. 'It'll all work out. Soon be the end of the term, anyhow. I'm just going to park the car. See you later?'

'I'm tired. I think I'll have a shower and off to bed. Thanks for everything, Frank,' she called softly as he walked round the car.

The front door she found was open and Miss Tucker was walking down the hall, her back stiff with disapproval. Had she heard Megan's farewell remark? Megan wondered as she hurried up the stairs and to the quietness of her flatlet.

CHAPTER VI

Megan was discussing the planning of the concert with Mr Taft when the letter came. It was delivered by hand, and she recognised Patrick's handwriting. It was a few days since she had seen him and she wondered if it was to say Georgina was worse.

'Will you excuse me, Mr Taft?' she asked.

The elderly man smiled at her. 'Of course— it might be urgent. I'll take a walk outside.'

He left her and went through the French windows to the terrace. What a beautiful sunny cloudless day, Megan was thinking, as she opened the envelope.

As usual Patrick's writing sprawled across the page. 'This is urgent, Meg. Georgina is worse and the doctor forbids her to dance. It means so much to me—better publicity, a more secure job, higher pay. Could you get Saturday off, come early so we can rehearse and you can take Georgina's place?'

Megan read it twice and then folded the letter slowly, her eyes puzzled as she frowned.

'Bad news?' Mr Taft, coming in from the

terrace, asked sympathetically.

'In a way,' said Megan. Saturday? That was tomorrow. Should she go? After all, Patrick was her brother. But how would Craig react? Or Miss Tucker?

'Look,' Mr Taft folded up his notes, 'suppose we postpone this for a few days? We have plenty of time and everything is going well.'

'Thanks a lot, Mr Taft. It's very good of you.' Megan still had the puzzled, unhappy look on her face.

She folded her notes and went out into the garden, as in a dream. Should she go and help Patrick? She knew she could dance nearly as well as Georgina. And if it meant so much to Patrick . . .

Deciding to ask Craig Lambert himself, rather than getting involved with Miss Tucker, Megan had to hunt for him, but he was nowhere to be found. No one knew where he was. Several of the staff asked her why it was so urgent. Megan had no answer for that, but she knew it was urgent, for she should ring Patrick and let him know if she could help him or not.

Suddenly she wondered if Craig was at his own house. She found Frank after tea and asked him to take her there.

Frank frowned. 'Is it a good idea, Meg? Lambert doesn't like his privacy invaded.'

'This is urgent,' she said. 'I think he'll

understand.'

'All right,' Frank agreed.

They drove in silence, for Frank had been there once.

'Only once, mind, in all these years,' he said as he deftly drove over the bad road, missing the huge bushes that grew close to the gravel and sending a small group of coloured parakeets screeching as they flew up out of the way. 'I'll wait in the car. I hope you know what you're doing.'

So do I, Megan thought, but she had a feeling Craig would understand. These last few days she had been expecting him to send for her, but he had seemed, she thought, rather to avoid her. Obviously Frank had convinced him of her innocence where Anarita and Gaston were concerned.

Megan stared at the lovely house as Frank stopped—the thatched roof, the huge windows, the garden bright with red and yellow roses and tall bushes that were a mass of cream flowers.

'I shan't be long,' she said.

Frank gave a funny grin. 'I hope I don't have to pick up the pieces!'

'Craig isn't like that,' she said as she got out of the car.

'That's what you think,' he told her. 'I wonder if you've met the real Craig Lambert yet.'

Feeling far from the braveness she was

172

posing, Megan walked down across the lawn. She paused, looking round her. There was the most lovely view . . . right over the bushes to the blue water. The lagoon was so quiet and still, the waves too far away to be heard. There was this quietness . . .

'What on earth . . . ?' Craig's annoyed voice broke the stillness and Megan swung round to find him frowning at her.

'Could I speak to you, please?' she said. 'It's urgent.'

'It must be. Is that Parr out there?'

'Yes. He said he'd wait in the car. I had to see you and I was afraid you might not come back tonight and . . .'

'You'd better come in,' Craig said. He didn't sound at all pleased and Megan followed him rather nervously.

She looked round, loving everything she saw, the oil paintings on the walls, the cream of the rugs on the polished floors, the deep armchairs and long couch, the French windows opening on to an enclosed garden with roses climbing up the brick walls and a tiny pool in the middle.

'Sit down,' Craig said curtly. 'What's the trouble this time?'

Megan told him, as briefly yet as completely as she could. She finished by saying: 'If he satisfies this man, it might mean a whole new life for Patrick. He'd go away, and that . . .well, surely that would please you?' she asked.

173

'Why does he want to leave the island?' Craig asked.

Megan hesitated. 'Well, he isn't happy here. He says there are too many frustrations, that . . . that things aren't working as he had hoped and . . .'

'His wife is too ill to dance? Can you take her place without practising?'

'If I could go in early tomorrow morning, I can. We'll rehearse all day. I expect Patrick will use the dances I know very well.'

'You did a lot in England?'

'Not so much recently. I did several years ago.'

'That was before your aunt left you?'

Megan nodded. 'Yes.'

'Did you mind? I mean, giving up the dancing?'

'In a way, yes,' she said, thinking back. 'I used to enjoy the dancing because it was a sort of challenge.'

'You miss it now?'

Megan was startled. 'I never think of it. That's just a part of my past life.'

'You'd like to do this dancing with your brother?'

She stared at the man facing her, his stern ugly face sympathetic. How was it so many people hated him? she wondered.

'Not very much, but . . . but if it would help him.'

Craig nodded. 'I thought as much. Well, you

have my permission. You can go, of course, early in the morning. I'll be going in, so I'll take you. I'll be coming over early to have breakfast at the school.'

Megan hesitated. 'Miss Tucker?'

'I'll settle that.'

'Thank you . . . oh, thank you so very much,' Megan said, and suddenly the words seemed to plunge out of her mouth, beyond her control. 'Thank you for being so understanding,' she went on. 'I'm awfully grateful. But I just can't understand one thing—why are you so much against the island coming up to date? I mean, it doesn't seem like you, somehow. You're so tolerant, so understanding, yet on this subject, you're . . .' She paused, but he said nothing, a faint smile flickering round his mouth, so she went on: 'Is it fair to the islanders? I mean, wouldn't they be better off if it was a big holiday island? Better wages and things? I mean, too, it needn't affect the school, need it?' She paused, wondering if she had said too much, but he looked amused rather than angry.

'I can see you've been brain-washed,' he said. 'Would you really like to see this beautiful island packed with Bingo halls, a casino, hotels? Don't you see that higher wages would mean that the locals would drink or gamble the money? Do you really think I'm indifferent to the people on the island? The school means a great deal to me, because I

175

respected my grandfather and think there's a need for this kind of school, though I do feel we're out of date in many ways and this must be revised in the near future. As regards the locals . . . we have sufficient schools and hospitals already. They are my people, so I supply these. Like my grandfather, I see the locals as my children and I shall do my best to protect them from the temptations of the so-called civilised world.'

'But . . . but shouldn't you trust them to resist temptation?' Megan asked. 'I mean, you won't always be around to protect them.'

'I agree up to a point, but they must first be educated enough to recognise temptation and its cost. The next generation will, I'm sure. This island was my grandfather's originally and one day it will be completely mine again,' he said firmly.

Megan hesitated. He wasn't at all angry, so she felt she could talk to him frankly.

'But is it really fair to them? I mean, they mightn't all of them gamble away the money, and those that wouldn't are being . . . well, deprived of the money they need and would use.'

He smiled. 'This is, of course, the problem. But isn't it better for a very few to suffer to save the lives of a great many? While I could keep account of the visitors to the island, we were safe. Today anyone could come in. That's what worries me—drugs, thieving, drinking too

176

much . . . it's changing the island already.'

'But hasn't change got to come?' Megan asked earnestly. 'I mean, isn't it progress?'

He stood up. 'Depends what you mean by progress. Obviously we have different versions. Poor Parr, sitting out in the car—I should have asked him in. Well, is that all right? I'll take you into town after breakfast.' Leading the way to the door, he spoke over his shoulder. 'Just one thing. Don't tell anyone—not anyone, not even Parr—about this. That understood?'

'Of course.' Megan stood on the white paving stones outside the front door and looked up at him. 'I don't know how to thank you for being so understanding.'

He gave a slight rueful smile. 'Sometimes I think I understand too well. See you tomorrow!'

Stepping back into the hall, he watched her hurry across the lawn to the waiting car, saw Frank leap out and open the door for her, and watched them drive away before closing the front door.

'Well?' Frank asked.

Megan laughed happily. 'He was absolutely super. I can't think why everyone is so frightened of him or else they hate him. I find him most understanding and kind.'

'You going to tell me what you wanted to ask him?' Frank enquired with a smile.

'No, I'm not. That's the condition, Frank.

Craig has agreed to let me do something, but no one must know about it.'

'I see.' Frank whistled softly. 'Very cloak and dagger!'

'Oh no, it isn't.' Megan laughed happily. 'It's much more to protect the school. Look, is there a phone box where I can speak without someone listening?'

Frank chuckled as he drove. 'I think there's one near the hospital. You've never seen it? Good, we'll go that way. You have a phone call to make? I needn't ask to whom? Gaston Duval, I imagine.'

'Then you're quite wrong . . .' Megan began, and her hand flew to her mouth. 'Now you're trying to make me talk, and I mustn't!'

Frank chuckled. 'My curiosity is aroused. I shan't be content until I know.'

'I doubt if you ever will know,' she told him triumphantly. 'I can see no reason why you or anyone should.'

One of the nicest things about Frank, she thought, was that he would accept things.

'You're dead serious?' he asked now.

She nodded. 'Dead serious.'

'Okay, let's forget it. Look, there's the hospital . . . can you see it?' He pointed to a long white building built on what looked like a plateau dug out of the side of the mountain. 'One thing about this island—we don't have to go to the mainland for surgery or anything. Lambert keeps good doctors and surgeons

178

here. There's the public callbox. Lambert had a bit of a row over having it put there, but as usual he got it.' Frank chuckled. 'He was right, too. You go visit a friend and he's worse, so you want to stay on, you have to call someone at home. You used to be able to phone from inside the hospital but somehow it didn't work. There were complaints that people used them socially.'

He parked alongside the callbox. Megan soon got through to her brother.

'I got your letter, Pat. I'm coming in immediately after breakfast tomorrow,' she told him.

'Great!' Patrick sounded pleased. 'How did you work it?'

Megan heard her voice go stiff. 'Mr Lambert consented—he realised this meant a lot to you.'

'How very kind of him,' Pat jeered. 'You really have got him on a bit of string, Meg. I wish you could talk some sense into him.'

Megan closed her eyes for a moment as she tried to keep her temper. Patrick was never satisfied. 'One thing, Pat,' she said, 'no one must know it's me. That understood?'

'Not know it's you? I don't get it,' said Patrick. 'Why not?'

'I don't know. Perhaps it isn't considered the right thing for the dancing mistress at the Lambert School to do exhibition dancing,' Megan said with a laugh. 'In any case, what

179

does it matter? The main thing is that I can help you out.'

'Right, Meg. I was thinking maybe we could make you look like Georgina. She's got a wig—anyhow, we'll see in the morning. Goodbye.'

'How is she?' Megan began, but Patrick had hung up the receiver.

She went out to the waiting car thoughtfully. Maybe that would be a good idea—wearing a wig to make her look like Georgina.

'Okay?' Frank asked with a grin.

'Okay,' she said. 'Look, Frank, I think I'll have an early night as I don't want to slip up and let anyone know.'

He nodded. 'I bet I could . . . make you slip up, I mean.'

Impulsively Megan turned to him. 'You really are a darling, Frank. I don't know what I'd do without you.'

He looked surprised and a little sad. 'We are good friends, aren't we, Meg?' he asked.

'Of course we are,' she told him. 'You're my very best friend.'

'Your best friend,' he repeated quietly as the car neared the school. 'I suppose I must be content with that.'

CHAPTER VII

That night, Megan found it hard to sleep. She couldn't forget the wistful note in Frank's strange words:

Your best friend. I suppose I must be content with that.'

What did he mean? Could he . . .? No, he mustn't, she thought unhappily, for he would only get hurt. She was very fond of him, in fact she loved him in a way, but it wasn't the way you loved when it meant marriage. That would be a totally different kind of love, the sort of love she felt for . . .

She made herself stop thinking, for she was suddenly afraid. She couldn't be in love with anyone, for there were two men in her life, and if you really loved anyone, there could only be one!

Each man meant so much to her, each man in a totally different way. When Gaston smiled, she felt wrapped in a warmth of happiness; when he talked to her, she found herself wishing he need never go. It was a strange love to her, if love it was. She found him fascinating—and yet at times she felt it must be purely a physical kind of love, not the real kind, for the real kind made you want to help him be happy, to look after him, stand up for him. Did she feel like that about Gaston?

What was the good of thinking like this? she asked herself, tossing and turning restlessly. It was a hot night and even the open, screened windows brought in only more heat. Maybe she should never have come out here, she thought, for whatever she did in the future she felt was bound to hurt her.

Marry Gaston? How could she? He must have made it up to please his mother, for he had made no attempt to meet *her,* Megan thought, or to get to know her better. But if he was serious . . . ?

Marry Craig? That was completely out of the question, for he would never see her except as a rather tiresome young person with whom he had to be patient!

But if . . .

She jumped out of bed and swallowed two aspirins, hoping they might send her to sleep, for her mind was on dangerous ground. Craig must not be thought of in that way . . . he must just be thrust out of her mind.

Finally she slept, and when she awoke and saw the clock, she leapt out of bed, for whatever happened she mustn't be late for breakfast! Luckily she sat next to Mr Taft who never asked questions, but she was startled when Craig suddenly stood up, walked down the room to her and said:

'Ready, Miss Crane?'

There was a sudden silence in the usually noisy dining-room and Megan knew that every member of the staff must be staring down at them, wondering why and where Mr Lambert was taking her!

As for the girls . . . Megan could guess how Anarita would be talking, for she loved to appear to know everything that no one else did.

In the car they hardly talked, but as they neared the town, Megan turned to the man by her side.

'I do appreciate you letting me do this, Mr Lambert. I told my brother that no one must know it's me. I think I'll be wearing a wig as he wants me to look like Georgina.'

Craig turned and looked at her, his eyebrows lifted. 'That won't be easy. She has a hard face.'

He left her at the Crane Dancing Studio. 'Good luck,' he said with one of the smiles that transformed his face. 'You have more courage than most girls would have. I'll arrange for you to be collected tonight,' he added as he drove off.

Megan hurried to the front door, but even as she went to ring the clanging bell, the door was opened and Patrick stood there.

'Good. I was afraid you'd fall out. We haven't danced together in years. We'd better get to work. We've got to be good.'

Where dancing was concerned, Patrick was not only a perfectionist but a hard taskmaster. She was quite exhausted when they stopped for a coffee break. Then she had the chance to ask how Georgina was and Patrick looked surprised.

'Didn't I tell you she was in hospital? The doctor doesn't seem to know what's wrong, so she's in under observation. That reminds me . . .' He hurried from the room and returned in a few moments with a dark wig, tossing it to Megan. 'Try it on.'

The wig was made in the elaborate built-up way Georgina's hair was set, but Megan couldn't even fit it on, for her own blonde hair was too long and thick.

Patrick, pacing the room impatiently, was annoyed. 'We'll get in Louis, he's Georgina's hairdresser, and see what he can do. I've also got a make-up girl and after lunch the dressmaker is coming to alter Georgina's dresses, because she's much bigger built than you and we can't have the dresses falling off.'

'Is the man here, Patrick?' Megan asked.

'The man?' Patrick looked puzzled for a moment. 'Oh yes, *the* man. Yes, he is. Now let's have another go . . . you weren't too good . . .'

Back to the studio they went, and Megan danced as she hadn't danced for years. In a way she was enjoying it. Patrick was a good dancer when he was in a good mood . . . but she decided she wouldn't like to be his permanent partner, for he had a nasty habit of shouting at her if the slightest thing went wrong.

184

They had a light lunch, then the dressmaker, a tall dark-haired woman, came, pursing her lips thoughtfully as she tightened Georgina's dresses so that they fitted Megan— beautiful, expensive, pearl-decorated dresses, one white, one green. Louis, the hairdresser, worked hard, but when he had finished and they all looked at Megan's reflection in the mirror, Louis shook his head sadly.

'I could never make you look like Georgina. You are too different, but you are both beautiful.'

Patrick said much the same, though not so politely.

'It can't be helped—we'll just say nothing to the man. He knows I dance with my wife and he may take it for granted that you are my wife, and if he's heard she had dark hair, we can always say it's dyed. Now . . .'

Back to work, and when the time came to bath and dress ready for the evening, Megan ached all over. It was only because she was out of training, she told herself, but all the same, she was glad this was a one-night show!

Everything was different when the moment came. The excitement raced through Megan's veins like magic as Patrick led her into the huge ballroom at the hotel, bowing to the audience while Megan curtsied. There were several flashes of light and she could see some of the visitors standing near the orchestra with small cameras. Then the music began . . .

It was the music that had the magic in it, the rhythm, the harmony, as they began to dance. She had no feeling of nervousness, no worry at all as she simply relaxed and let the music lead her.

Afterwards as they bowed again and again to the roar of applause and clapping, Megan seemed to come back to life. It had been like a dream . . .

'You are so good a dancer,' exclaimed Gaston, coming to stand close beside her, taking her hand in his and kissing it. He looked round, but Patrick had vanished. 'You are so much better than Georgina. You should be Patrick's partner. You will dance with me?'

The orchestra had begun to play again and gradually the great empty floor was getting covered with dancers. Gaston took her in his arms and they danced.

Megan felt his cheek brushing hers, the way his fingers curled round her hand. He turned his head to smile at her.

'My mother—she told you?' he asked.

'She told me what?' Megan hedged for time, for he had startled her.

'That we are to be wed.' He smiled almost triumphantly.

'But that's absurd . . .' she began.

'Why is it absurd?' he asked as the music stopped and they came to a standstill. She saw that he had danced her off the main floor and they were standing in a quiet deserted corner near the bar. He kept his arm round her, turning so that they stood side by side as he bent and kissed her.

Even as he did, there was a sudden flash of light, and Megan pushed him away.

'What was that?' she asked sharply.

Gaston frowned. 'What was what?'

'That light . . . it flashed.'

'Probably a car outside. It happens as they park.' He pulled her close to him again. 'Tell me, Megan, why is it absurd? You will not marry me, is that what you say?'

'Look, Gaston . . .' Suddenly Megan knew beyond a shadow of doubt that though Gaston had a strange effect on her, it was not love. 'I don't know you and you don't know me.'

'We could learn to know one another. It makes my mother happy,' Gaston began, his face breaking into the smile that must, Megan thought, have broken the proverbial thousand hearts.

'That's why you want to marry me, isn't it?' she asked him.

He looked startled, his arm falling down. 'You are suggesting . . . ?'

'Miss Crane?' Craig's deep authoritative voice interrupted them. 'There you are. I couldn't find you. I've come to fetch you.' He came striding across the end of the room towards them.

Gaston moved forward. 'It is far too early. The evening has not begun.'

Craig looked at him with contempt. 'The evening, as far as Miss Crane is concerned, is over. I agreed to her dancing with her brother.'

'But not with me?' Gaston smiled. 'You are her guardian?'

'No, I'm her employer. Collect your things and change, Miss Crane. My car will be outside the Studio.'

Megan hesitated as she looked from one man to another. It was the first time she had seen them together and the difference in them was almost amazing. Craig, a well-built man with his square chin and high forehead, his short dark hair, dark eyes and that ugly yet handsome look, made Gaston look like a university student with his long curly hair and that strangely fascinating smile. Craig was a man, but Gaston . . .

'Yes, Mr Lambert,' she said meekly, 'I'll be as quick as I can.'

She turned and hurried out of the hotel and into Patrick's house, went to the guest room where her clothes were, hastily changed, removed the make-up and brushed out the carefully curled hair.

Craig was in the car when she went outside. He didn't speak as he drove away and then abruptly, without looking at her, said:

'Your dancing was superb. I wonder Patrick didn't make you his partner.'

Megan turned eagerly. 'You saw us?'

'Of course. Unfortunately I came in a little

late, so I missed the first dance. He's a good dancer, too, your brother.'

'He's a perfectionist. I wouldn't like to work for him. Maybe that's why he and Georgina keep quarrelling—he's so convinced he's always right.'

A smile hovered round Craig's mouth. 'Maybe he is.'

Megan laughed. 'Maybe, but he needn't shout about it.'

'Did the man you said would be there say anything? I mean, offer him the job he wants?'

Shrugging, Megan shook her head. 'I have no idea. As soon as we stopped dancing, Patrick vanished and . . .'

'Gaston Duval took over,' Craig said drily. 'Is he serious?'

Startled, Megan looked at him. 'Serious? Oh, I see what you mean. He says he is, but I think he's only saying that to please his mother.'

'His mother?' Craig's voice changed. 'You've met her?'

'Yes, the other day. It seems Gaston wrote and told her he was going to marry me.'

'Marry you?' Craig's voice rose. 'Are you out of your mind?'

Megan laughed a little uncertainly. 'Of course not. It's just what he says, that he wants to marry me, but I don't think he does.'

'Then why?'

'Because, as I said, he wants to please

Madame Duval. She's English.'

'I know. I met her many years ago when I was a schoolboy—a beautiful woman, but hard as nails. Gaston is an only child and very spoilt.'

'That's what she said . . .' Megan stopped abruptly as she glanced at him. 'She said he was like Patrick, and I think she's right. Patrick can get anything out of my father, anything he wants.' She added wistfully: 'Dad never loved me. He just makes use of me.'

'He may be the type of man who finds it difficult to show emotion.'

'He shows plenty over Patrick,' Megan said bitterly.

'So when young Gaston told you he was going to marry you, what did you say?' Craig's voice had changed, was almost accusing.

'I said it was absurd, that we didn't know one another and . . . well, then you came along.'

'And had I not come along?' They were nearing the school now as Craig asked that.

Megan looked at him. 'I'd have said the same. I don't even know him.'

'But you find him very attractive?'

'Well . . .' she hesitated. 'He is rather fascinating . . . that smile and . . . but that isn't love,' she added solemnly.

'It isn't?' Craig drew up outside the school front door and turned to look at her. 'Then what is love?'

190

'I . . .' She looked round her, anywhere away from his eyes that seemed to be looking right into her mind. How could she tell him the truth—the truth she had known as Craig stood by Gaston and she could compare them—the truth that she loved Craig, loved him with every single inch of her. 'Loving is wanting to make a person happy, to feel the person needs you.'

'A romantic idealist!' Craig sounded amused. 'You're very young,' he added, getting out of the car and walking round.

But she was too fast for him, battling with the car handle but getting out as he reached her. *You're very young,* he had said. Just as she had thought and feared, that was how he saw her.

Fortunately she was so exhausted physically that her worried thoughts failed to keep her awake and she was asleep almost as soon as her head touched the pillow. In the morning, her body ached a little and her limbs felt stiff, but it was Sunday, so there wasn't much to do. She managed to avoid the rest of the staff. After lunch she slipped away to sit with her book in a shady corner, sheltered by great rocks balanced perilously on one another, the shade supplied by the palm trees. But she couldn't read. She sat, her hands clasped round the book as she gazed blindly into the distance.

Now she was in real trouble, she told

191

herself. There was no doubt in her mind whatsoever—it was Craig she loved.

Could there be anything more impossible than that? First of all, there had been her impossible dream of the island, and she had found it. Now there was the impossible dream of being Craig's beloved wife . . . What hope had she that such a thing could ever come true?

Craig saw her as a very young person. It was not a passionate or exciting description. A young person he was sorry for and very patient with . . . not the sort of woman he would seek to be his wife.

What sort of woman would he love? she wondered. Someone with a husky voice and beautiful features like Petronella Weston?

It was four days before she knew. And as it was in a time of shocked surprise, the knowledge didn't help in the least.

It all began with a curt order from Miss Tucker to present herself immediately, so Megan hurried to the headmistress's room. As she entered, she saw that Craig was standing by Miss Tucker's side, both silent as they watched Megan walk across the room.

Never had the room seemed so long, never had Megan felt so nervous, for never had she seen Craig look like that . . .

He held out a newspaper. 'Look!' he said curtly.

Megan's hands were trembling as she

obeyed. She caught her breath with dismay, for it was the island's newspaper and on the front page were two photographs. One of her dancing with Patrick—the other of her in Gaston's arms as he kissed her.

The headlines were: *Famous Lambert School's Dancing Mistress finds Romance.*

'I . . .' Megan looked up, horrified, unable to speak.

'I told you that no one was to know you were taking part in the exhibition dancing, Miss Crane.' Craig's voice was cold as ice, it seemed to cut its way through her. 'You knew they were taking photos?'

'I saw a few flashes. I thought it was the hotel's guests.' Megan's hand flew to her mouth. 'I did ask Gaston what it was, but he said a car's head-lights as it parked. I had no idea. I told Patrick that no one was to know.'

'A likely story!' Miss Tucker chimed in. 'The harm you've done to the school since you came! You should never have . . .'

'Miss Tucker, kindly leave this to me,' Craig snapped.

The headmistress looked as if she was about to explode, but she moved back, sat down and waited.

'I told Patrick . . .' Megan said. 'He told me he wanted the man to think I was Georgina . . .'

'Your name is there,' Craig snapped. 'Georgina, it seems, is in hospital. This is not

193

the type of publicity we're seeking. I . . .'

Megan was very close to tears. 'I'm terribly sorry, Mr Lambert. It was awfully good of you to let me help Patrick, but if I'd thought anything like this would happen . . .' She stopped speaking, pressing the back of her hand against her mouth. 'I had no idea . . .'

'I don't know what to say,' Craig told her slowly. 'I trusted you.'

'I told you not to. We don't want girls of that calibre here. I told you from the beginning that she was most unsuitable, quite apart from her being mixed up with those dreadful people,' Miss Tucker exploded.

'That's all, Miss Crane,' Craig, ignoring the angry woman by his side, said curtly. 'I would suggest that for the next few days you remain in your flat. I'll arrange for food to be sent up. It will give you a chance to complete the dancing programme for Mr Taft.'

'Stay in my flat?' Megan, feeling stunned, echoed.

'Yes,' he said curtly. 'We may get journalists here and I don't want you to make things worse.'

Megan looked at him, her eyes filling with tears. 'Please believe me,' she said. 'I had no idea, no idea at all. If I had . . .'

The tears were so horribly near falling that she turned and ran, hurrying across the hall and up the stairs, going into her flat and flinging herself on the bed.

How could Patrick have been so wicked? So cruel? So selfish—for this would mean the end of her job. She wouldn't be asked back next term, that was for sure, she thought as she wept.

But worse was to come, for on the third day Miss Wilmot arrived, coming to see Megan in her flat.

'Miss Wilmot?' Megan said, delighted to see someone who would break the miserable loneliness she was suffering, and went forward eagerly to greet her, but stopped dead as she saw the anger on Clare Wilmot's face.

In her hand were several English newspapers as well as a French one. 'The harm you've done with these photographs—and the news,' she said. 'Parents are ringing me from all over the world. This isn't the sort of publicity they or we want. How could you behave so badly? It was good of Mr Lambert to give you the job in the first place, despite your unfortunate relationship with Patrick Crane and Gaston Duval. How could you do this to him?'

Suddenly the most awful thing happened, for Clare Wilmot's composed, beautiful face seemed to crumple and she sank into a chair, her hands hiding her face.

'How could you . . . how could you do this . . . to Craig?'

Megan stood stiffly and silent. So Clare, too, was in love with Craig?

'I knew nothing about it, Miss Wilmot. I told Patrick I was allowed to help him but that no one must know and . . . I don't suppose you believe me,' Megan added.

Miss Wilmot lowered her hands. Streaks of mascara ran down her cheeks. 'Lambert School means so much to Craig—I know that. I know, too, that it needs to be modernised, that Miss Tucker must go, but Craig's heart is too soft about her. She's due to retire next year, so he wanted to wait until then . . . but this . . .' Clare Wilmot touched the newspapers. 'Goodness only knows the harm you've done. Gaston Duval is known everywhere as a jet-set playboy, kissing every girl he meets. I'd have thought you'd have had more sense. How can we trust the girls with you? As for letting them photograph you . . .'

'I didn't . . .' Megan bit her lip. No one would believe her. She knew that. No one at all, least of all Graig.

'Look,' Clare Wilmot's voice changed, became almost wheedling, 'the best thing you can do is to resign and leave the island. Craig won't want to hurt you. But if you go, he'll be glad. You're nothing but a nuisance. In any case, when I come out here permanently, I wouldn't keep you. I consider you're far too young. Next year, when Miss Tucker goes, I'm going to be headmistress. Craig and I will run the school together.'

Megan began to see light—and she didn't

like what she saw.

'You and Craig . . . ?' she said slowly.

Clare Wilmot nodded. She went to the mirror and cleaned her face, speaking over her shoulder.

'Of course. We've known for years, but there was no hurry. We're still young.'

'And . . . and you think I should resign?'

Clare Wilmot swung round, looking pleased. 'It's the only solution. Write a note to Mr Lambert and I'll arrange for your flight back to England. There, that's not too bad,' she said, peering closely in the mirror. 'Goodbye,' she added, leaving the flat.

Megan stood very still, her hands pressed to her face. Yes, now she came to think of it, Clare Wilmot was the sort of woman Craig would marry. Beautiful, dignified yet efficient, witty, friendly yet firmly sure of herself in every way, she would make a perfect wife.

Suddenly the tears won and Megan flung herself on the bed, hugging the pillow tightly, as she cried. Why, oh, why had she ever come out here? she asked herself miserably. It could only lead to heartache. It had already led, and there was nothing she could do about it. Nothing at all.

CHAPTER VIII

Megan had to face up to the truth: Miss Wilmot was right. There was only one thing to be done. Megan knew she must hand in her resignation.

Craig was too kind-hearted to do it himself, but, as Miss Wilmot said, he would be glad to be rid of the dancing mistress who had caused so much trouble!

Looking at the clock, Megan saw that soon her lunch would be brought to her on a tray. If she wrote the letter quickly, she could give it to whoever brought the tray and ask her to take it straight to Mr Lambert.

It wasn't an easy letter to write. In fact, she crumpled up three attempts until finally she decided it was the best she could do.

'Dear Mr Lambert, I am sorry I have caused so much trouble. I hope you will believe me when I say I didn't mean to. I can't help feeling that the best thing is for me to leave the school, so may I hand in my resignation? I am sorry, as I am very happy here, but I really do think it is the only thing I can do.
Yours sincerely . . .'

She signed it, re-read it to make sure her

spelling was right, and then found an envelope. She had just sealed it when there came a knock on the door and Odette brought in her tray.

'Please give this immediately to Mr Lambert,' Megan asked.

Alone again, Megan had no appetite at all and she played with the food. So that was that . . . the end. The end of her dream, the end of everything.

Now she would have to plan what to do next. Miss Wilmot said they would fly her back to England, and once there, what sort of job could she get without proper training? What kind of reference would Craig give her? Perhaps she could go back to Mrs Arbuthnot in Hastings.

She went out on to the balcony and breathed in the warm fragrant air. How still the lagoon was. She turned to look at the mountains that dominated the island. How she loved it all, and soon she would see it for the last time as the schooner took her to the mainland and the waiting plane.

There was a knock on the door, so, thinking it was Odette again, Megan called: 'Come in!'

She was startled to see as the door opened that Craig stood there. He pushed the door to behind him and came towards her, her letter in his hand.

'What's this nonsense about?' he demanded.

'I . . . I thought you'd like me to go.'

'It has nothing to do with me liking anything,' he told her impatiently. 'If I allow you to leave it will look like an admission of guilt, and I don't believe for a moment that you were to blame for what happened.'

Megan clasped her hands tightly. 'I'm most grateful. Please . . . I honestly had no idea.'

'I know you hadn't. I've told you before that you're a rotten liar. Sit down.' He jerked a chair out from the side of the table and straddled it.

Megan sat down slowly on the edge of the armchair, holding herself stiffly as she waited.

Craig stared at her. 'Do you think your sister-in-law was really ill?' was the first question he shot.

Megan was startled. 'Yes, I did . . . I do think so. I've never seen her look like that before. Her hair was in an awful mess and her face very white.'

'Well, there is such a thing as make-up. I've just phoned the hospital and they say she's been discharged and that there's nothing wrong with her.'

'I can't understand it. That's what her doctor said, but honestly . . . honestly, she looked dreadful. So pale and . . .'

'I see. As I said, there is such a thing as make-up, of course,' he said drily. 'It was obviously a plot designed by someone to cause bad publicity to the Lambert School. You agree?'

Megan nodded miserably. It could only be the truth.

'Unless . . . unless the photographers were there because Mr . . . Mr . . .' she paused.

'You mean the important man your brother wanted to impress? What was his name?'

'Yes.' Megan hesitated, for she didn't know it.

'Was there such a man?' said Craig. 'Or was your brother playing on your sympathies?'

Megan brushed her hair back with her hand.

'I don't know,' she confessed. 'I didn't think it at the time, but . . . but now you ask me, I do remember saying to Patrick something about *the man* and he—Patrick, I mean—said something like "The man? What man . . . oh yes, the man." I thought then it was rather odd. As if he . . .'

'As if there was no man at all. That's what I believe. I must say the whole thing seems to me like a woman's scheming. What about your sister-in-law? Was she eager for you to take her place as her husband's partner?'

'We didn't talk about it. You see, when I saw her, it was several days before she was taken to hospital. There was no question then of my taking her place.'

'Do you think she would have minded?'

Megan sighed. 'I honestly don't know. When I went there to rehearse as I said she had gone. I know she wasn't very keen on impressing the man.'

'She mentioned him, then?'

'Yes. She said Patrick was more concerned with the man's opinion than with her feeling so ill. She doesn't want to leave the island. She loves it here.'

'I see.' Craig looked thoughtful for a moment, gently tugging at his ear. 'Was Madame Duval there at the time?'

'Gaston's mother?' Megan asked, then felt uncomfortable because of the way Craig looked at her. 'Yes. I was with Georgina when Patrick came and told me I had a visitor. I went with him, and that was when I met Madame Duval.'

'How did you get on with her?'

'I rather liked her. She was most friendly.'

'And very bitter about me, of course.'

'Not really, just resentful, because she feels it couldn't make any difference to you letting Gaston make money here.'

Craig gave a little grunt. 'Sometimes it's convenient to be blind to the truth. I wouldn't trust her. Like most mothers, she's completely amoral when concerned about her children. They don't want the school to stay here. They want to close it down and have the whole island to themselves. They think that if they make life impossible for the school—and they've done their best in the past with anonymous letters and malicious gossip—I might go back to my real work and sell them the island.'

'Your real work?' Megan asked.

His face relaxed a little. 'I'm an archaeologist by desire. I gave it up when my father died and I had to come here to take over. This is my responsibility. I respected my grandfather very much. He was good to me, understanding and stepping in where my father wouldn't bother, so I felt I owe it to my grandfather to do my best to keep his ideal of a school going. Of course, as I've said before, we must change quite a few things here. I plan to start that next year . . .' He frowned suddenly. 'I mustn't waste time chatting like this.'

He stood up and looked at her thoughtfully. 'I think everything has been smoothed out now and even the irate parents have accepted Miss Wilmot's diplomatic letters.' He smiled. 'She's an amazing person. I often wonder what I'd do without her.'

Megan thought that what Clare Wilmot had said must be the truth. Next year, Miss Tucker would go, Craig would marry Clare and they would modernise the school.

Craig walked towards the door. 'Only ten more days before the end of the term, so we'll return to the routine.' He looked at his watch. 'How time flies! Look, Frank Parr is going into town tomorrow as he's having trouble with his new glasses. I suggest you go with him and call on your brother.' At the doorway, he paused.

'You might shock him into truthfulness for once,' he added as he went out.

Megan stood up, standing very still, her hands pressed to her face hard. So now what? She was staying, but . . .

For how long? Next year when Miss Wilmot became Mrs Lambert and took over, the first person to be sacked would certainly be Miss Crane!

However, now she was free to return to her usual duties, so she hurriedly changed her dress and went down into the school, seeking Mr Taft as she had been studying his notes and there were several questions. He was friendly as usual and no reference was made to her behaviour. Dinner time would have been a nightmare, but Frank took care of her, sitting her between himself and Mr Taft. No one spoke to her except them; in fact, she had a strange feeling of not being there because it was so obvious that Petronella Weston and the other staff had decided to stay far from her in case they got involved!

Afterwards, Anarita came up, her dark hair swinging, her lovely face happy.

'We threatened to go on strike, Miss Crane, when we heard you were housebound, but Mr Lambert explained it was to protect you from the journalists. Miss Crane, it was such fun. There were journalists and men with cameras and it was just like war, we weren't allowed out so we waved from the windows . . .' She

204

laughed happily. 'Are you going to town tomorrow with Mr Parr? I know he's going, only I'd like to go, too.'

Megan hesitated, very conscious that several members of the staff were looking at her disapprovingly, they were probably afraid that some of her 'wickedness' might come off on poor Anarita.

'It's rather awkward, Anarita. You see, I was going to see my brother and . . .'

Anarita laughed. 'He's out of bounds as far as I'm concerned. Right? I only like going with you, Miss Crane. The other girls get lifts in, but I wanted to wait for you.'

Megan smiled. 'That's nice of you. Look, why not ask Mr Lambert yourself? Say I wasn't sure if he'd agree?' She looked round. 'There he is. Come on, I'll go with you.'

Craig was standing on the terrace, talking to Petronella Weston. He turned with a frown as Megan and Anarita went up to them.

'Well? What is it this time?' he asked.

Anarita spoke first. 'Could I go into town tomorrow with Miss Crane?'

'Of course you can,' Craig said irritably. 'You always do.'

'I wondered . . .' Megan began.

Craig scowled. 'Don't wonder, just do what I say. I told you life had returned to normal.' He turned away, almost rudely.

Anarita giggled as they walked away. 'He's in one of his moods! Anyhow,' she gave a little

205

skip, 'that'll be nice. See you tomorrow, Miss Crane,' she said, and danced away to join her friends.

Megan returned to her flat. She felt she didn't want questions, comments—or what was even worse was being sent to Coventry, which it seemed to be what most of the staff were doing.

Tomorrow . . . but how was she to see Patrick if Anarita was with her? Could she ask Frank to chaperone Anarita for an hour or so? It was all so old-fashioned, Megan thought restlessly. Yet she remembered she had been told that girls in Spain and Italy are chaperoned even today, so perhaps it was wiser in a school where there were so many different types and nationalities to be on the safe side.

The next day Anarita was waiting by the car when Megan joined her. Frank was sitting behind the wheel, listening to Anarita's chatter. Not that it stopped once they were in the car, for Anarita seemed thoroughly miserable.

'I've just heard, Miss Crane, that I've got to stay here for the hols. I'm so mad! I thought I'd be going to Rome this time, but my aunt is ill and none of my other relations will have me, so my guardian says I must stay here . . .'

Megan, twisted round in the front seat so that she could talk to Anarita, smiled. 'Is that so terrible?'

'It certainly is. At least it will be this time. There are only eight of us and the others are kids—no one of my own age group. Are you going to stay for the hols, Miss Crane?'

Megan was startled. Somehow she hadn't really worried about it, but it was a problem. If she didn't, or couldn't, stay, where could she go? Certainly not to Patrick's. She felt so angry with him that she knew there was going to be a really big row. She had done her best to help him and what had he done in return? Made her look an absolute heel, someone not to be trusted, someone cheap and nasty. If it *was* Patrick, of course, but the more she thought of it, the more she felt Craig was right, for who else could it have been? Patrick had talked of *the man,* had said Georgina had to go to hospital, and he must have known about the photographers and given the press her name, although she had told him that no one must know she taught at the Lambert School.

The car was approaching town as Anarita leaned over the side, pointing towards the jetty. 'Look, Mr Parr, isn't that the schooner? I didn't know they came on Saturdays.'

'They don't usually,' said Frank, swerving deftly to avoid a herd of goats strolling across the road. The small pastel-painted houses were coming closer now and they could plainly see the jetty going out into the harbour. 'There was a breakdown of some kind, so it didn't go yesterday.' He glanced at his watch. 'It'll probably go about four o'clock or a little later.'

'Look, Miss Crane,' Anarita said excitedly. 'There's a baby monkey on his mother!'

'So there is,' said Megan, a little puzzled, for they were always seeing monkeys and as a rule Anarita ignored them. 'Got some shopping to do, Anarita? I want some toothpaste and some air mail letter forms.'

She should write again to her father, she knew, though he never bothered to answer her letters. But he would have seen the headlines in the papers and perhaps even her photographs, and might be wondering what she was up to. If he cared, that was, she thought unhappily.

Frank dropped them, as usual, just below the noisy colourful market and Megan led the way to the post office, Anarita following meekly by her side.

As they left the post office, they met Tracy Thompson, the artist, in his trendy gear.

'Hi!' he said in his friendly manner.

Anarita turned her back and strolled a few steps away to pretend to look in a shop. Megan frowned. Even if Anarita preferred older men, that was no excuse to be rude.

'Hullo,' Megan said friendlily. She liked this hippie-type artist, for he had good manners, and she liked his long curly brown hair that was so clean it shone in the sunlight. 'How are things?'

'Not too bad,' he told her. 'I'm pretty lazy.

Not used to this heat. It makes me sleepy when I should be painting.' He glanced at Anarita's back and looked at Megan with a wry smile. 'Why is she mad at me?' he asked.

Megan laughed. 'At the moment, she's mad at everyone. I'm sorry she's like it.'

'An adolescent temperament,' Tracy said with a grin. 'Be seeing you!' He walked away, merging into the crowd.

Megan joined Anarita. 'There's no need to be rude,' she scolded.

Anarita laughed. 'You don't know that type. Give them a smile and they're after you. I don't like being pinched.'

'But he's not Italian.'

'It isn't only Italians who pinch,' Anarita said with a sigh of exasperation that made Megan feel about sixty years old.

'Let's . . .' she began, and stopped, for— blocking their path—Gaston Duval and his mother stood.

'My dear child!' Madame Duval exclaimed, holding out her hands as she looked admiringly at Anarita. 'You remind me of your mother. She was a beautiful woman, too.'

Gaston's hand was under Megan's elbow. She shivered a little and he obviously took it as encouragement, for his fingers tightened, digging into her flesh.

'Let's have a cold drink,' said Anarita. 'I'm thirsty.'

'But . . .' Megan began, then paused. Back

to normal, Craig had said, so how could she refuse to let Anarita have cold drinks with people she had obviously known for years? She could see no choice, so she walked with them to the café, then they sat near the road, under a green and white sun-umbrella.

Gaston talked to Megan. 'What a tyrant, that man of yours is, is he not?' he asked her. 'The way he has no manners, at all. We had danced but once, and . . .'

Megan drew a breath. If he was involved in the conspiracy he had no right . . . But was he involved? That was the question.

'I heard Georgina was discharged from the hospital as being perfectly well,' she said, her voice sharp.

Gaston shrugged. 'The hospital, they are perhaps mad. Like her doctor. But who is the one to know the pain? I say to Patrick, this is a serious matter. Take her to the mainland. Go and find a proper doctor.'

'I was told the doctors here were very good.'

'Good!' Gaston said scornfully. 'What is good on this island?'

Angry, yet not wanting to make a scene there in public, Megan turned to Madame Duval, and found to her amazement that Anarita and Gaston's mother were talking in Italian.

Madame Duval, who had looked a little depressed, Megan had thought, seemed to have changed completely. Her face had brightened, her eyes were sparkling. She even clapped her hands, nodding her head so that her small mountain of white hair swayed gently. Then she seemed to remember Megan and turned quickly.

'I'm sorry, my dear. How very rude of us, talking Italian when I know you can't speak it.' She smiled at Anarita. 'You're just like your mother, my dear—full of bright ideas. I hope it works out. And what did Mr Lambert say about your portrait in the paper, Miss Crane?' Madame Duval asked, her voice amused.

'He wasn't at all pleased,' Megan said, her voice controlled. 'Nor was I.'

'Ah, but why? It was just a warning . . . to our friends, perhaps?' Madame Duval chuckled happily. 'You're staying for the holidays, Anarita? I shall be here. Maybe you could come to me?' She looked enquiringly at Megan who had caught her breath. 'What do you think, Miss Crane?' Madame Duval continued. 'You too, for I imagine you've got nowhere to go? That would be very nice, wouldn't it, Gaston?'

'But of course,' he said quickly with that special smile of his, but this time it left Megan completely cold. 'We would have fun, that I am sure.'

'I imagine Anarita's guardian would have to be consulted,' Megan said coldly.

She saw the quick look that Gaston and his mother exchanged, so she went on: 'Anarita, I

211

have some shopping to do, so we must go. If you'll excuse us, Madame Duval.'

'So soon?' Madame Duval looked disappointed and then she smiled at Anarita. 'But perhaps it is not too soon.'

Finally Megan managed to get Anarita away and they walked down the street towards the market. 'We're much too early, you know,' said Anarita.

'I know, but . . .'

Why don't you like me meeting the Duvals, Miss Crane?' Anarita asked. 'They're nice people.'

'I know, but . . .' Megan hesitated. What could she say? Then she had a bright idea. 'I think Mr Lambert is afraid you'd fall in love with Gaston.'

'That layabout?' Anarita's scorn was harsh and startled Megan. 'He lives off his mother and likes to think every girl falls for him. Well, I'm one who doesn't. I like my men . . .'

'To be older?' Megan laughed.

Anarita paused outside one of the big bazaars.

'Let's go in here. I hear they have some super silk scarves,' she said. 'Down at the end.' She pointed to a crowd of plump Creole women in their bright dresses, all talking at the top of their voices, laughing happily, standing round a table.

'It's a bit of a crush . . .' Megan began, holding back, but Anarita caught her by the hand.

'Come on, Miss Crane. We just push like they do!'

The scarves were there. They were silk, and beautiful colours. Megan picked one up in her hand to look at.

'Isn't it lovely, Anarita?' she said to the girl by her side, turning to look at her.

Her heart seemed to skip a beat, because Anarita wasn't there! Dropping the scarf, turning round, trying to push her way through the crowd of women, Megan tried not to feel frightened, for surely Anarita was only playing her favourite game again? But it was a nightmare, as she forced her way through the groups, trying to find the girl, but she wasn't in the bazaar, Megan was certain finally. Outside the bazaar in the hot humid air, she shook back her hair and looked up and down the street. Anarita was just having a rather stupid joke! She would find her demurely waiting for Frank and his car.

But Anarita wasn't there. Frank was, though, and Megan told him quickly what had happened.

'Not again?' he said, and frowned. 'Honestly, Meg, I'd have thought you'd have more sense!'

Megan's eyes stung. That was hard coming from Frank. What would Craig say?

'Anarita would go in the bazaar and there were so many people there, but it all happened

213

so quickly. I spoke to her and looked round and she wasn't there . . .'

Frank frowned again. 'That child needs a good spanking. It's not my idea of a joke.'

'Nor mine.'

'Look, Meg, you search down that side of the street and I'll do this side. I'll bet she's hiding somewhere just to see us looking worried. All that girl wants is attention.'

'And love,' Megan put in quickly.

'She doesn't deserve love when she deliberately gets you into these messes. We've asked her so many times not to get lost,' snapped Frank, sounding exasperated.

'I know. Well, I'll try this side,' Megan said miserably.

It was hard going; fighting to get into a shop, fighting to walk round, looking everywhere, and then another fight to get out, so when Megan met Madame Duval walking slowly along the pavement, she almost ran to meet her.

'Have you seen Anarita, Madame Duval?' Megan asked, her face flushed and dusty, her hair hanging listlessly, her eyes tired.

'Anarita?' Madame Duval smiled. 'I saw her go with you.'

'I know she did. We went into a crowded bazaar and . . .'

'She vanished?' Madame Duval sounded amused. 'Girls of that age have a weird sense of humour. Her mother was much the same.

We wouldn't think it funny, but she did. How she would laugh and . . .'

'I'm terribly sorry,' Megan said desperately, 'but I'm afraid I must look for her.'

'But of course,' Madame said with a smile.

As she left her, and pushed her way through the noisy crowds, Megan wondered why Madame Duval looked so amused. To Megan, it was not funny, not funny at all. Craig had been so patient with her, so tolerant—but if she had really lost Anarita this time, what would he say?

At the end of the street, she stopped. She couldn't see Frank in sight. Perhaps he had worked his way down faster than she had. She saw a public telephone box and on an impulse hurried into it.

She got through to the Lambert School with blessed quickness, but the slightly sing-song voice of the young clerk who handled the school's switch-board irritated her.

'No, I don't want Miss Tucker,' Megan said, again and again. 'I want Mr Lambert. It's urgent.'

'Urgent? You are hurt?' the girl asked, sounding alarmed.

Megan gripped the earpiece. Whatever happened she mustn't cause a panic. 'No, I just want to speak to him. It's important. Tell him it's Miss Crane.'

'Oh, Miss Crane, of course! I didn't recognise your voice!' the girl said, her voice

215

implying that only people like Miss Crane would make such a frenzied call. 'I'll try and get him.'

Megan waited, as patiently as she could, aware that several people were queueing up outside and looking annoyed so that when at last she heard his voice she spoke impulsively.

'Oh, Craig, thank goodness it's you! I'm so worried. Anarita has vanished.'

'Vanished?' he echoed, sounding annoyed. 'But you told me she often does it as a joke. Why this panic?'

'Because I don't think it's a joke. I think it was planned. She chose the most crowded bazaar and we . . . she led the way through the crowds. Looking back, I think I . . .'

'Have—as usual—made a mess of things,' Craig said coldly. 'All right, I'll come out right away. Meet you at the market. By the way, you're not to tell anyone that the girl has vanished. Understand?'

'Yes, but . . .' Megan began, but heard the receiver slammed down and replaced hers slowly. She had told Madame Duval. What would Craig say when he knew that?

*   *   *

Actually, to Megan's surprise, Craig took the news that she had told Madame Duval very well.

He had arrived at the market at the same

216

time that Frank had joined her, looking irritated as he shook his head.

'No sign of the kid, Meg,' Frank had said. 'When I get my hands on that girl, I'll . . .' he began, even as Craig's car drew up.

Craig leant out of the window. 'Both get in sô we can talk,' he said curtly.

Megan and Frank obeyed. Craig drove a little further away to find a parking place, then turned and looked at her.

'Start at the beginning. What happened?'

Megan drew a deep breath. 'Well, we . . . we were walking along and . . .' She hesitated. Was it necessary to mention Tracy Thompson? She decided not, for it had no bearing on the subject at all. 'We met Madame Duval and Gaston and they insisted on us having a cold drink. Actually it was Anarita's idea.'

Frank groaned softly and Megan looked at him.

'How could I refuse without being rude?' she asked. 'After all, Anarita has known both Gaston and Madame Duval for years, ever since she was a child.'

'Go on . . . you had cold drinks with them,' said Craig. 'And then?'

'Well . . . well, I was a bit worried as I wasn't sure how you'd feel about us being with the Duvals, so I said we must go to meet Frank . . . er . . . Mr Parr. Anarita pointed out afterwards that it was much too early and she'd heard that a certain bazaar had some wonderfully cheap

217

things. We went in there. I tried to stop her, because it was so crowded, but she just went on, so I kept close to her. I was looking at a scarf and she was by my side, and then . . . then I turned to speak to her and she was gone.'

'Just like that?' Craig asked. 'How long were you looking at the scarf?'

'Only a few minutes,' Megan said desperately. 'I hunted all through the bazaar and couldn't find her, and then I saw Frank and he said we'd do one side each. It was then I bumped into Madame Duval, so I asked her if she'd seen Anarita and . . . I'm awfully sorry,' she said again, looking at Craig worriedly. 'If I'd known you didn't want anyone to know I wouldn't have told her.'

Much to her relief and surprise, Craig smiled.

'It was natural for you to ask if she had seen the girl, so don't worry about that. I understand Anarita often plays this trick on you?'

Frank spoke first. 'She does, and I gave her a real talking-to, threatened never to bring her in again if she did it once more. I know how it upsets Meg.'

'Naturally. Was Anarita her usual self today?'

'She was very depressed. It seems she'd hoped to go to Rome for her holiday and had just heard from her guardian that she had to stay at school,' Megan said.

218

'Why did she mind so much? She's often stayed at school.'

'She said all the other girls were little kids. Could she have run away?' Megan asked.

Craig frowned. 'I doubt it. No clothes and no money—as far as I know, that is. Did you get that impression?'

'We did notice the schooner was in the harbour,' Frank said. 'And she was interested. That right, Meg?'

'Yes, she seemed surprised. Oh!' Megan's hand flew to her mouth. 'Something else I forgot to tell you. When we were having cold drinks with the Duvals, Gaston was talking to me and then I found Anarita and Madame Duval were talking in Italian. I wondered what it was about, because Madame Duval seemed very pleased about something. When we first met her, she had been quiet and rather . . . well, miserable, if you know what I mean, but after talking to Anarita Madame Duval changed cornpletely. She even told Anarita she was like her mother, full of good ideas.'

Craig sighed. 'Look, I'm afraid this is a matter for the police. You'd both better come with me as you were the last to see her.'

'The police?' Megan was suddenly frightened. 'You think she's in danger?'

Craig shrugged. 'Anything can happen. That girl is my responsibility and as such, must be found. Whether she's run away of her own accord or been kidnapped is neither here nor there. She has to be found.'

'Kidnapped?' Megan almost whispered the word. 'Who'd kidnap her?'

Craig looked at her, his face seeming to be made of stone, it was so hard and cold.

'I wouldn't put it past your charming Madame Duval,' he said. 'As I told you, she'd do anything to get the island.'

'You mean the ransom could be the island?' Megan said very slowly. 'Do you really think they'd do that?'

'I don't know. Look, Frank, you follow us in your car. After we've seen the police, you take Megan back to the school. You're neither of you to say anything. If asked where Anarita is, say she's visiting friends and will be fetched later. However, you'd better tell Miss Tucker the truth. Understand?' Craig's voice was harsh. He looked at Megan. 'That goes for you, too. Also tell Miss Tucker *no one* must know. Right?'

'Yes. I'm so awfully sorry . . .' Megan's voice was unsteady.

'I should have known better than allow her to come in with you,' Craig said as Frank hurriedly left them, running back to where his car was parked.

The police turned out to be courteous, but Megan got very tired of repeating the same story over and over again. Of course they were trying to trip her up, she thought, they had to make sure she was telling them the same each

220

timc. Well, she was. She was telling the truth.

Frank drove her back to the school and both hardly spoke. Megan had the uncomfortable feeling that, for once, Frank blamed her for her carelessness, so it was a relief when, nearing the school, he smiled at her.

'Don't look so frightened, Meg. That kid'll be all right. It wasn't your fault. She can take care of herself.'

'You think she ran away?'

'I think she's trying to frighten us . . . well, look, you know Anarita. She loves publicity. I wouldn't mind betting she's hiding somewhere in town and will let the press have some extraordinary story.'

'I hope you're right,' Megan said miserably. 'Now we've got to look normal. What do we do about Anarita?'

'I think we'd better see Miss Tucker,' Frank said with a rueful grin, 'and get it over.'

It was an unpleasant interview, with Miss Tucker's cheeks and nose getting redder and redder, her voice more and more unsteady.

'We should never have engaged you,' she said angrily to Megan. 'Never, in the past, have such things happened to us.'

'It wasn't Miss Crane's fault,' Frank said.

Miss Tucker glared at him. 'How can we trust you, either? You might both of you be in this. Never—ever—have we had such a scandal. One of our girls kidnapped!'

'Miss Tucker,' Frank chimed in, 'Anarita

may not have been kidnapped. She may have run away.'

'Why should she run away from a school like this?' Miss Tucker was indignant. 'She was happy here.'

'She wasn't,' Megan said. 'She resented lots of things—especially having to spend the holidays here.'

'That's absurd! The girls have a pleasant time. In any case, that's beside the mark. Anarita was in your care, Miss Crane, and you have failed to stand up to the responsibility entailed. This is the final thing. I shall speak most sternly to Mr Lambert about you . . .'

'Mr Lambert said no one must know, Miss Tucker,' Frank said, looking towards Megan. 'He made that very plain. No one—but no one—must know,' he added, his voice hard. 'We're only telling you. If anyone asks where she is, Mr Lambert says we're to say she's visiting some friends and will be back later.'

'Will she?' Miss Tucker said bitterly, twisting her hands together. 'If she isn't killed. That would be the end of everything. Never has this school . . .'

'Come on,' Frank said quietly to Megan as Miss Tucker walked towards the window, talking angrily, but as if to herself. 'I'll see you at dinner,' he said quietly. 'Remember we have to act as if nothing had happened. Probably they'll have found Anarita by then, so try not to worry.'

'I'll try,' Megan said, smiling at him but seeing his face through a blur of tears.

Alone in her flat, she saw the letter waiting on the table. It was from England, the writing faintly familiar. She opened it. The letter was from her father! She began to read it eagerly, but her pleasure became dismay as she read what he had written.

'I was horrified to see your photo in the Sunday newspaper. What sort of people are you associating with out there? In any case, I think you must come back. Your Aunt Lily's health seems to be deteriorating and you know I can do nothing, so the sooner you're back the better.'

Megan read it several times, puzzled. Somehow it didn't read like her father's normal speech. Maybe he was ill, too. Perhaps the arthritis had affected his hands, because the writing was odd, too. Go back? Was it her duty to go back if her father needed her? She went out on to the balcony. The blue lagoon was still, its lovely colour in the late sunshine strikingly beautiful. Go back? Go back to nurse Aunt Lily and her father, to listen to their perpetual quarrels, to know that nothing she could do would ever be right? Yet he was her father, after all.

Megan dreaded the dinner, but Frank, as usual, helped her through it and, as few of the staff had decided yet to talk to her, there were no awkward questions. There was no sign of

223

Craig, though, and that worried Megan very much. Surely if Anarita was just trying to frighten her or, perhaps, tease her—for somehow she couldn't think of Anarita wanting to hurt her—surely if that was all it was, Anarita would have been found by now?

Later, walking outside with Frank, talking quietly, Megan reminded him how once she had told him that she had the strangest feeling with Anarita that she was playing a game that Anarita was winning, and that Anarita, in addition, was aching with the desire to tell Megan all about it.

'I know that sounds involved, but . . .'

'I understand,' Frank said thoughtfully. 'But why should she want to play a game with you? No point in it if you didn't know you were playing it.'

Megan sighed. 'I just don't know. So long as she's all right . . .'

'I'm sure she is,' said Frank. 'Quite sure.'

Megan looked at him. 'I wish I could feel as sure!'

She hardly slept that night and, waking with the dawn, she got up, quickly dressed and slipped down out of the school and then on down to the edge of the lagoon. There was a pathway alongside the water and she knew it could not be many miles. She *had* to do something about it all—had to face up to Patrick and Gaston and Madame Duval to make sure they were not in it.

224

She reached the town at last and found her way to Patrick's Studio of Dancing and to his house next door. Ringing the bell, she waited until the door was opened by their manservant, Victor. He looked startled.

'Mr Crane? Tell him it's his sister,' Megan said, and walked into the house and straight to the lounge.

It was quite a few moments before Patrick joined her, tying the belt round his dressing-gown, blinking sleepily as he gazed at her.

'What the hell do you want at this hour?' he demanded.

'Is Anarita here?' Megan said.

'Anarita?' He looked puzzled. 'Oh, Anarita.' His face broke up into a big smile. 'Of course she's not. Why?'

'The police are looking for her,' Megan said, and watched his face but he showed no dismay or fear. Ought she to have told him, she wondered, yet surely if Madame Duval knew, then it was certain she would have told Gaston and Patrick. 'They think she may have been kidnapped.'

'Kidnapped? I wish we'd thought of that,' said Patrick. 'We could have asked for a fortune or the island!'

'Then someone has kidnapped her!' said Megan. It was as if a hand was clutching at her throat, making it hard for her to breathe.

'What on earth . . .' Georgina said sleepily as she came into the room, wearing a very

225

elegant silk housecoat. 'What are you doing here, Meg?'

Megan looked at them both. 'How could you be so mean!' she said angrily. 'You lied about being ill, Georgina. You lied about the man wanting to see you dance, Patrick. You lied about everything to get me in that mess.'

Patrick grinned. 'So what? It worked, but not as well as we hoped. Maybe this time we'll do better.'

'What do you mean?' Megan's voice quivered a little. 'You've kidnapped Anarita?'

'Of course we haven't,' said Georgina. 'Patrick hadn't the brains to think that out. All the same, it's nearly as good. It'll be in all the papers today.' She smiled maliciously. 'Headlines, I expect. Famous heiress, pupil of the once-renowned Lambert School, has disappeared. Kidnapping is feared. How much ransom will be demanded? It'll be as good as if it had really happened. What do they say? *There's never smoke without fire.*' She laughed. 'Your fine Mr Lambert will be wiped out!'

'But . . .' Megan began, and paused.

Patrick was laughing. 'A bit of luck, that was what it was. Gaston and his mum bumping into you and the girl saying she was going to elope . . .'

'Elope?' Megan's mouth was dry. 'With Gaston?'

Both Patrick and Georgina laughed. 'Not on your life!' said Patrick. 'It's that artist chap

'. . .Tracy something or other.'

'Tracy Thompson?' Megan gasped, finding it hard to believe.

Georgina laughed. 'Sure. That's what she told Madame Duval. They've known one another for years, it seems, and have got tired of waiting for her to be twenty-one. Anyhow, Megan, I guess you'll be looking for a job soon, because that school will crash.'

'You . . . both of you!' Megan was so angry, she couldn't speak. She looked round her wildly, at the expensive furniture that the money they had talked her father into giving them, had paid for. She turned and rushed outside into the street, then hurried to where she knew was a taxi rank. It might cost a lot, but she must get back to the school as soon as possible.

As she arrived, she ignored the startled gaze of several of the staff who came down to breakfast early.

'Miss Tucker,' Megan, not realising how flushed and untidy she was, hurried to the headmistress. 'Is Mr Lambert here?'

'No. He's at his house.' Miss Tucker frowned.

'Why?'

'I've something to tell him. Something important.'

'You can use the phone in my office, then,' Miss Tucker said, looking rather worriedly at the girls who were all talking loudly and laughing as they ate. 'Some news?' she asked softly.

Megan nodded, her honey-coloured hair swinging forward, and she pushed it back. 'I think it could be good news,' she said.

She soon got through to the house—the house she loved.

When she heard Craig's voice, she reminded herself to remember that the girl on the switchboard might be listening.

'Mr Lambert?' she asked. 'I've . . . I've seen my brother and . . .'

'You have something you wish to discuss with me?' Craig Lambert's voice was crisp. 'I don't want to come in just now and this is a good place to talk, so I'll send my car in to fetch you,' he added curtly, and she heard the slam as he put down the receiver.

Not in a very good mood, she thought, as she hurried up to her flat, to brush her hair, make up her face, and put on a clean dress. There were clouds piling up in the sky. She wondered if there was a storm brewing up.

She was in the hall when she saw, through the open door, Craig's car. She hurried out before anyone could stop her or even ask her where she was going but as the chauffeur opened the car door, Megan looked up at the school and saw Miss Tucker and Petronella Weston standing at a window, gazing at her. They looked pleased in a strange way. Perhaps, Megan thought, they saw this as the end of her. Even Craig's tolerant patience could not be tried too far and surely this time he must be so angry with her that she was bound to leave? Megan, sitting in the car, shivered. They would be glad to see her go. Neither had liked her, right from the beginning. In fact, she had only two real friends at the school: Frank and Mr Taft.

Craig was walking in the garden in front of his house as she reached it. He came slowly to meet her. His face seemed blank, as if he was wearing a mask. He waited for the car to drive round the back and then looked seriously at Megan, who was finding it hard not to tell him her news.

'Well? You wanted to see me?' he asked coldly.

'I think she's all right.' The words now fell out of Megan's mouth. 'I saw Patrick and Georgina and it was all done deliberately—the other business, I mean. You were quite right . . . but I wanted to know about Anarita and they told me she had eloped.' She paused, breathless, staring at him, as they walked slowly across the grass.

'I know,' he said.

It was a shock. 'You know, and you didn't . . .' Megan began.

Craig lifted his hand. 'I was about to ring you when you rang me. I had just heard from the police that they traced Anarita and her boy-friend to the Mainland, but don't know where they are now. Judging from the description I imagine it's Justin Newell.'

'It isn't,' Megan said eagerly. 'It's Tracy Thompson. He's an artist and we used to see him in town . . .' Hurriedly she told Craig about their occasional meetings with the hippie-artist. 'I liked him, but Anarita wouldn't speak to him. She said she preferred older men.'

Craig's stern face creased into a smile. 'How naïve can you be?' he asked. 'Naturally she didn't want you to guess that she and this lad were deeply in love!'

'You knew?' Megan stood still as she stared at him.

'In a sense, yes. She and Justin have been in love since she was fourteen, but naturally her guardian refused to treat it seriously. He declared it was adolescent infatuation. We argued about it, because I felt that Anarita was too mature and too eager for life to be happy at our school, but her guardian, Jerome Hardwick, was adamant. However, he agreed that if they stayed in love for several years, he might relent. It's a pity you didn't tell me about this artist.'

'I . . . well, it didn't seem necessary, because Anarita just ignored him. I wonder . . .' Megan's eyes widened as she thought of something, 'I wonder if they used to have secret meetings when I lost Anarita? That would explain . . . but yesterday when we met him, she moved away and wouldn't look at him. I wonder if they decided to elope on the spur of the moment? Because Anarita didn't want to spend the holiday here.'

'I'm not really surprised,' said Craig, his mouth amused. 'She'd have no chance of seeing him, because there are few staff here in the holidays and I doubt if Anarita would get a lift into town at all, and that would have spoilt everything. After all, the lad only came to the island in the hope of meeting her occasionally, I imagine.'

'The schooner was there,' Megan said eagerly, then paused, her face clouding. 'But I'm forgetting the worrying part. They've . . .' her mouth was dry, 'they've—and I think Patrick meant Madame Duval—sent the news to all the papers that Anarita has been kidnapped. That'll be dreadful for you . . . Madame Duval thinks it will ruin you completely.'

'I guessed they'd do something like that.' Craig pushed open the front door and they left the humid fragrant air for the cool air of the hall. 'So I got through myself to London. Pity Miss Wilmot wasn't there at the time, because I could have contacted her. However, the newspapers know it was a hoax. That there never was any question of kidnapping and the romantic story of the seventeen-year-old girl who after four years of waiting has eloped with her love will be the *real* exciting news, because

231

Justin is heir to an even greater fortune than Anarita, so from that point of view her guardian has no reason to disapprove. I think he'll accept the fact that their love is sincere and give them his blessing.'

He led the way to his book-lined study and asked her to sit down, then got them both iced drinks.

Megan could feel the tenseness leaving her body slowly as she relaxed in the chair. Everything was going to be all right? When Craig sat down on the other side of his desk she said eagerly:

'Then . . . then they can't hurt the school?'

He smiled. 'For the moment, no. Next week is end of term. Next term . . . well, let's hope we'll have no repetition of this term's unfortunate incidents.' His voice seemed to have grown hard.

Megan fumbled in her handbag. 'I think it would be best if I leave. I seem to have brought you nothing but bad luck.' Her voice wavered for a moment, wishing he would deny it, but he said nothing, just went on watching her. 'I . . . My father wrote to me and wants me to go back.' She passed over the letter.

Craig read it silently and then looked up. 'You want to go?'

Megan shook her head violently, then stopped. She hadn't meant to react like that! 'He is my father. Perhaps I should.'

Turning the letter over slowly in his hands,

232

Craig said:

'Were you surprised to get the letter?'

'Very. My father hasn't written to me once since I've been here.'

'You've written to him?'

'Of course.' Megan hesitated, but Craig seemed sympathetic, so she went on: 'I was surprised when it came. It's so unlike him. I mean, he's always been impatient with people who use long words. He says short words are good enough for him, but in this he's used long words. Another thing, I really wondered if perhaps his hands are bad, because the writing isn't like his was . . .'

'Just a moment,' Craig interrupted. He stood up and went to a tall filing cabinet in the corner of the room, pulling open a drawer and taking out a folder. He went back to his desk, turned the pages of the papers before him and brought out a letter. 'I see what you mean,' he said slowly. 'There is a slight difference in the writing.'

'When did my father write to you?' Megan asked, half rising, but Craig gestured to her to stay where she was, so she sank back in the chair.

'He didn't.'

'Then how have you got a letter of his?'

Craig leant back, folding his arms, looking at her with a slightly supercilious smile.

'It really began several years ago when your brother moved in on the island. Naturally I had to find out if he was a genuine dancing teacher or if this was some drug-taking project. I had his background looked up in England, and this included his father and sister.'

'Wasn't that . . . well, you . . .' Megan hesitated.

'Look, I'm responsible for these girls and their lives, for their parents trust me, therefore I'm careful. I already knew all about Gaston Duval's past, his mother's determination to get the island for her beloved son but Patrick Crane was a new personality, so I had to find out all I could about him. What I found out reassured me. He had a clean background, had always taught dancing and danced. Georgina was the same—you too. So I did nothing to stop your brother from opening the Crane School of Dancing. Indeed, I could see nothing wrong in it—until he became more deeply involved with the Duvals. I knew then that they would stop at nothing, that the ridiculous feud between the Duvals and Lamberts would never end. I began to distrust your brother. I see I was right.'

'But if you doubted Patrick, why did you engage me?' Megan asked. 'Did you think I was involved in some way and want to keep me under your eye? That reminds me . . . what about Frank and Miss Tucker? Shouldn't they know Anarita is all right?'

'They do. I rang up soon after you'd rung me and told them.'

'Miss Tucker and Petronella watched me leave.'

He smiled. 'I expect they looked pleased?'

'They did,' Megan said bitterly. 'They've never liked me—nor has Miss Wilmot.'

'No . . . I can understand that.' Craig turned over the letter still before him. 'In a way, though, I find it utterly deplorable.' His smile softened the last word.

'I suppose they know you're going to sack me?' said Megan. 'That's why they looked so pleased.'

'I did give them that impression,' Craig told her.

Megan clenched her hands together tightly. She didn't want to go. Never to see him again? And yet she knew it was the only answer.

'I . . . I don't seem to have been much help to the school, I'm afraid,' she sighed.

'On the contrary, you've been of great assistance,' Craig told her. 'You've opened my eyes to many things. Also the way the Duvals have behaved has put them in my power. I shall now be able to sue them . . . or threaten to, and believe me, Madame Duval will be off this island and take her son with her within seconds. She can't bear the danger of her name being involved. She's a very proud woman and she loves her son and will always give him money . . . but it ends there. I think they'll recognise that they've lost the battle, for nothing, not even the destruction of the

235

school, will make me leave the island.'

'But I must go,' Megan said slowly.

'Yes,' Craig told her. 'You must go.'

CHAPTER IX

Megan knew that it had to come. She had expected it, though she had steeled herself for when it came, but all the same it hurt her terribly. Fortunately for her, giving her time to overcome the shock, the phone bell shrilled at that moment and Craig answered it.

As she sat, dazed, yet knowing it had to be accepted, for she could see no other solution, she realised suddenly that Craig was talking to Anarita.

'Yes, it *was* naughty of you. Poor Miss Crane was very upset . . . I understand. I know, it wasn't her fault. Thank you for telling me, Anarita. You phoned him? Good girl . . . very sensible!' Craig was nodding, smiling as he spoke. 'He agreed? I'm glad. Yes, I'm sure she'd love to. What was that?' he asked, and nodded. 'Yes, you can speak to her. She's here with me now.' He held out the phone to Megan. 'Anarita would like to speak to you,' he said.

Megan stood up, moved nearer the desk and took the phone in her hand. 'Anarita?' she said.

Anarita's excited voice drummed in her ears as she listened to her apology.

'I hadn't planned to go, Justin was willing to wait, but knowing I'd be there all the holiday and hardly see him was just the end, Miss Crane. Then seeing the schooner in seemed that fate was playing with us, so when I skipped out of the bazaar and met Justin . . . I bet you've guessed that I always met him when I got lost?' Anarita laughed happily. 'I said to him, let's get out of here, and he agreed. We just caught the schooner at the last moment. Luckily I had my passport with me. I always carried it as I knew one day we'd get tired of waiting. You can imagine how we felt! Anyhow, I phoned my guardian and he says we can get married. Isn't that super?'

'Wonderful, Anarita,' Megan said warmly. 'I'm so glad for you. I wish I'd known.'

'How could I tell you?' Anarita asked. 'You'd have had to tell Mr Lambert and he'd have had to stop it, wouldn't he? Anyhow, Uncle Jerome is planning a big wedding for us in about a month's time. He insists on that, and I was wondering, Miss Crane, if you'd be one of my bridesmaids?'

'Me, a bridesmaid?' Megan was startled. 'I'd love to, but . . . well, I don't know where I shall be.'

She was even more startled, for Craig had moved, come round the desk to stand by her side, and put his arm round her, leaning down

237

to speak into the receiver.

'Don't worry, Anarita, she'll be there. I'll see to that,' he promised.

'Thanks, Mr Lambert.' Anarita's laugh was gay.

Megan handed the phone to Craig and tried to move away, but his arm tightened round her. She stood very still, willing herself not to tremble, fighting hard to hide her misery.

'*You must go,*' he had said earlier on. '*You must go,*' and though she had known it had to happen, it was still too terrible to accept. But how did that fit in with her being a bridesmaid?

He was talking. 'Don't worry, Anarita. Yes, I know it's in all the papers, but I've sent news of your elopement. They knew, though . . .? You what? You told the Press? I see. You wanted it all to be above board.' He chuckled. 'You certainly twisted poor old Hardwick's arm. He was only concerned for your good, you know. Yes, we are old squares, I agree, but I don't agree with your statement that we don't understand. Believe me, we do. And it's just as painful for us. Right, Anarita. Thank you for phoning, and I'm glad everything is working out so well.'

He put down the phone and looked at the girl standing so still in his arms, her face drawn and miserable, her cheeks very white. He moved away and saw how slowly she walked to her chair and sat down. He went behind his

238

desk.

'This letter,' he said, lifting it in his hand. 'Forget it, Megan. Your father didn't write it.'

Megan's face came to life. 'You don't think he did?'

'I'm sure he didn't. As I said, comparing it with this other letter of his, I'm sure he didn't. In any case, last week my man in England went down to Dorset. I wanted him to check. It was a bit of luck,' Craig smiled, 'but he got lost just outside your Aunt Lily's cottage. Your father was working in the garden . . .'

'But he always said he couldn't,' Megan began.

Craig smiled. 'I can imagine. Anyhow, he and my man had quite a talk. Your father is very happy, it seems. Your Aunt Lily, too, is well and putting on weight.'

'So I needn't . . .' Megan began, and stopped. Her father didn't need her. No one did.

Suddenly she realised something. 'But if my father didn't write the letter, who did?'

'Miss Wilmot.'

'Miss Wilmot?' Megan gasped. 'But you and she . . .'

Craig smiled. 'She may think so, but I've never given her cause. So many women indulge in wishful thinking . . . as you know,' he added.

Her cheeks were hot. Had she *indulged* in it, she wondered, and did he know? Was this a

239

not-so-gentle hint?

'But Miss Wilmot said . . .' she began.

'Ignore what Miss Wilmot said. She has always, unfortunately, been jealous and possessive, and this is the last straw. I find it hard to understand how she could be so foolish—she's stuck one stamp from another envelope. This letter was written *here.*' He frowned. 'There are going to be big changes. I've decided to make them at once. Miss Tucker must go. I'm arranging for her to retire a year earlier than normal, but I shall make this financially better for her. Quite a few of the staff will go, including Petronella Weston, who has extremely annoyed me with her behaviour.'

'Miss Wilmot said *she* was to be headmistress.'

'Miss Wilmot?' Craig threw back his head as he laughed. 'That really is absurd! She hasn't a clue about children. No, I'm offering the job to Frank Parr.'

'Frank?' Megan was startled. 'Headmaster of a girls' school?'

Yes. It happened at Roedean, didn't it? I can trust Frank, he has a good sense of humour, tolerance, he gets on well with both staff and the girls and he isn't handsome enough for them to have crushes about him.'

'Frank is . . .' Megan began quickly.

Craig chuckled. 'Standing up for someone, as usual, Megan? I know Frank has *something*

240

. . . that's why I'm offering him the job. I hope he'll take it. Think he will?'

Megan leant back in her chair, half-closing her eyes, remembering the long talks she had had with Frank, how often he had told her he was against too much discipline. 'It should be self-discipline,' he had said. 'I trust children and then they are to be trusted. It's laying down ridiculous rules that causes rebellion and friction.'

Megan nodded slowly as she looked at Craig. 'I should think so. He'd be a wonderful headmaster.'

'Are you in love with him?'

The unexpected question was a shock. 'No . . . I'm very fond of him, but I definitely don't love *him*.' She realised with dismay that she had emphasized the last word. She could only hope Craig hadn't noticed.

'Good. Perhaps I should say, not so good for Frank. He loves you. You know that, of course?'

Megan nodded. 'I'm sorry, but . . .'

'Don't get a guilt complex about that, Megan. It's not your fault. Where was I? Oh, yes, there'll be a real re-shuffle of the staff. I'll be consulting with the new headmaster and then . . .'

'And then?' Megan almost whispered the words.

'I'm off to South America.'

'South America?' she repeated. That was

thousands of miles away, she thought, dismayed. He would go right out of her life for ever . . . but perhaps that was better. It might be less painful than seeing him every day and knowing he saw her as a young nuisance!

Suddenly she thought of something and her hand flew to her mouth. 'What about Patrick?' she asked nervously. 'I think he has . . . well, I think it was the meanest . . .'

Craig looked amused. 'Your brother is weak and easily influenced. Gaston Duval has a smooth tongue and built up a wonderful future with the minimum of work. I think Patrick realises life is not as simple as that. He's been made a good offer for the dancing school, one I think will tempt him so that he'll sell it.'

'And go back to England?'

'I doubt it very much. Actually I'm buying the Studio of Dancing myself and shall offer him the post of manager. I'm also going to arrange for the classes of older girls to go to his school for lessons. I shall arrange, or have arranged,' he added with a smile, 'for them to meet more people, lead a more normal life. Patrick could be of assistance in this way.'

'You're very good . . . 'Megan said slowly. 'Not many men would be so kind.' It seemed as if everybody's life was being wonderfully arranged except her own! she thought sadly.

'South America is a wonderful continent,' Craig went on, his face thoughtful. 'I told you I was an archaeologist by preference? Well, it seems something interesting has turned up in Brazil, so I'm taking a six-months' holiday. That'll give Frank time to find his feet before I come back. I want him to be able to manage on his own, but this . . .' he waved his hand round expressively, 'will always be my home.'

Megan nodded. She couldn't tell him, but she would give anything for it to be her home, too, she was thinking, when Craig startled her, by leaning forward over the desk and saying:

'Brazil is an ideal place for a honeymoon, you know.'

The words sank into her mind slowly. For a moment she could only stare at him, but then, somehow, she forced herself to speak.

'So you're getting married?'

'I hope so. If the girl will have me,' said Craig.

'The girl?' Megan whispered, for what girl would keep him waiting for an answer?

He picked up something from the desk, walked round and bent over her.

'This is the girl. Do you think she'll say yes?' he asked, showing her a photograph.

Megan caught her breath. It was a photograph of herself!

'But . . . but . . .' She looked up and found he was bending so close to her that his mouth was very near. 'You love me?' She sounded startled.

He nodded. 'Ever since my man in England sent me this. I think he took it when you were shopping in the supermarket. He sent photos of the three of you—you, your father and your Aunt Lily. I like to know everything about people I'm going to have to trust. I took one look at this photo of you and the strangest thing happened.' He was smiling as he spoke. 'Frankly, I've always been rather sceptical about love, Megan, particularly love at first sight. Yet, as I said, I looked at your photograph and knew you were the girl I wanted to marry.'

'But . . .' Megan felt confused, for this was so unlike the Craig Lambert she had known. 'You mean you fell in love with my photograph?'

He laughed. 'I did. I don't mind telling you it was a bit of a shock. However, I knew I had to meet you and get you to know me—for I felt I knew you already.'

'Then it was because of me that poor Miss Pointer was sacked?' Megan asked.

'Yes and no. Miss Pointer would have been sacked much earlier but for you. She was always a bit of a rebel; grumbling about the school, making the girls discontented because of our stringent rules. I had, for some time, been thinking of firing her, and then you turned up and when I learned you were a dance teacher, it seemed the answer. So I went and met your Mrs Arbuthnot and told her I needed a teacher. I managed it so that we talked about you. I asked if I could see some of

244

her teachers at work and she was only too willing to show me. I said I thought your youth and originality was what we needed . . .'

'It wasn't really?'

He smiled. 'Actually, it was really, but at the same time I wanted to get you out here so that you could get to know me. I could hardly ask you to marry me when you hadn't even seen me, could I? Anyhow, your Mrs Arbuthnot agreed you were a good teacher and she said frankly that she wished you could have the job as she was very concerned about you. However, she told me it was unlikely that you would ever have a chance of accepting such a good job because of your loyalty to your father. That seemed to block off all my efforts. Still, I refused to give up hope. Your father wasn't all that old, maybe he'd marry again. You were young and I would have to wait. So I let Miss Pointer stay on. Then I heard your father was selling the house and that you were looking for a job.'

'Craig . . .' Megan stopped him, her eyes narrowed as she thought. 'You didn't deliberately make Patrick . . .'

He looked startled. 'You don't really think I'd . . . ?'

'I don't think so, but they said . . .'

'If you'd rather believe what they said.' Craig sounded hurt and turned away.

'Craig, please,' Megan said quickly, 'I didn't think that, only it seems such a coincidence
245

that Patrick should ask Dad for money and Dad sell the house so I was free and . . .'

Craig turned round again, smiling. 'Not a coincidence but fate, Megan.' He pulled her gently to her feet and clasped his arms round her loosely. 'I jumped at the chance I was offered and got you here. Tell me,' his arms tightened slightly, 'tell me the truth—do you love me, Megan?'

It was difficult to think properly when she was so close to him. She shook her head slowly. 'I can't believe you love me, Craig. It was just one of my dreams that I knew could never come true.' Somehow her arms found their way round his neck as she looked at him. 'Surely you can see!' she said with a smile.

'I still want you to tell me,' he insisted.

'I can't realise it, Craig. I just can't believe it. You . . . well, I had no idea you felt like that about me,' she almost whispered.

'I couldn't let you know in term time, could I? I was waiting for the holidays. But like Anarita, I refuse to wait any longer.' His arms tightened. 'Megan, will you be my wedded wife?'

'Oh, Craig, of course I will!'

'You still haven't told me.'

She laughed happily. 'It's like a fairy tale. My dream of an island with palm trees and blue lagoons, and a house with a thatched roof, and the darlingest man in the world . . .'

'Megan . . .'

Megan stroked his face gently. 'Of course I love you, Craig. I love you very much indeed.'

'That's all I wanted to know,' Craig said as he tightened his arms so that she could hardly breathe.

At that moment, the phone bell shrilled impatiently.

Craig laughed. 'Let it ring. I've more important business to do,' he said, and then he kissed her.